Love
AT THE
SHORE

Based on the Hallmark Channel Original Movie

TERI
WILSON

Hallmark
PUBLISHING

For more about the movie, visit:
www.hallmarkchannel.com/love-at-the-shore

Chapter One

*S*UMMER, HERE WE COME.

Jenna Turner stood with her arms crossed, studying the loaded trunk of the SUV. It was parked in the driveway of the cozy home she'd made for her family deep in Savannah's Victorian district. She was just about ready to say goodbye to the surrounding trees dripping with Spanish moss and the rows of tidy houses dolled up in gingerbread trim. A temporary goodbye, anyway.

If the crammed state of her car was any indication, there wasn't anything left inside her year-round home to pack. Just how much stuff did one adult and two kids need for five weeks at the beach?

All of it, apparently. All of the stuff.

Why did she get the feeling she was going to need a vacation to recover from all the packing and unpacking involved with moving into a beach house rental on Tybee Island? A vacation from her vacation.

She somehow wedged the antique typewriter that once belonged to her grandfather into the small space between her laptop and printer. It fit. Sort of. Jenna flashed a triumphant grin at her best friend, Maureen, who was making her way over from the house next door.

Maureen and her family were also headed to the beach for summer break. But as usual, while Jenna was strategically packing and organizing, Maureen strolled across the lawn as if she didn't have a care in the world. Jenna envied her cute new summer wardrobe, in colors that perfectly complemented Maureen's smooth dark complexion. She also envied her friend's go-with-the-flow personality. Jenna's own tendency to plan everything down to the finest detail could get a little exhausting. A lot exhausting, if she was really being honest.

"Hey," Jenna said, giving the typewriter another shove.

Maureen aimed a bemused glance at the packed trunk. "Hey."

"Every year we say we're not going to bring too much, and every summer we're bursting." Honestly, it was mind-boggling.

"If you wouldn't insist on bringing that thing..." Maureen pointed at the typewriter.

"That *thing* may look like a dusty old antique, but it helps me brainstorm when I'm stuck. And considering I only have five weeks to finish my book, I need it." She crossed her arms again and tried not to think about how quickly five weeks could pass. She could do this. She *had* to. "This whole sequel thing is much more difficult than I thought."

A sequel. Her second book contract. Sometimes she had to give her arm a little pinch to remind herself that she'd actually written the book with her name on the cover currently sitting in the window display of her favorite bookshop on River Street.

Maureen grinned. "Then it's a good thing you'll be spending all summer with me for inspiration."

"Absolutely." Jenna laughed, despite the gnawing sense of panic that came over her whenever she thought about her deadline.

Maureen was right. They had the whole summer to look forward to—nothing but sun, sand and writing. It would be relaxing and productive, just what she needed.

"Hi, Maureen." Nick, Jenna's eleven-year-old son, bounded out of the house with his younger sister, Ally, hot on his heels.

"Bye, Maureen." Ally waved as she and her brother made a beeline for the car.

Jenna held up her hands. "Wait, wait,

wait: final check. Nick, did you grab your retainer?"

He nodded. "Yes-th, it's in my mouth."

"Please don't pretend-lisp." Jenna lifted a brow at the suspiciously empty-looking backpack hanging from her daughter's slim shoulders. "Ally, did you get your summer reading?"

"You can just call it homework, Mom."

"As long as you have it, sweetie. We can work on semantics later." She was almost certain the books were packed in Ally's luggage somewhere. Ally had always been a big reader, and now that she was nine years old, she'd begun devouring chapter books from the local library.

Given Ally's sweet tooth, she'd probably reserved her backpack for the brownies Jenna had baked last night for their road trip.

"Can Grayson ride with us?" Nick shot Maureen a hopeful grin. Her son Grayson was Nick's closest friend.

"If any of us were actually packed, yes." Maureen sighed.

Nick and Ally piled into the backseat, which meant Jenna had approximately ten seconds to get behind the wheel or Ally would break out the brownies.

Still, she felt bad leaving her friend behind. "You sure you don't want us to wait for you?"

4

"As much as I'd love to get my hands on your super-neat packing skills, you remember last year?" Ah, yes. Maureen's husband, Ian, had spent nearly an hour trying to make room for their gas grill in the trunk of their car alongside their suitcases. It never fit. "And the year before?"

"Yeah." Jenna winced. The year before, there'd been a similar delay involving a giant inflatable beach ball.

Maureen nodded, and her eyes danced with laughter. "We're a slow-moving team."

Accurate. But as usual, Maureen seemed as calm and unruffled as a yoga teacher.

"You're right. We'll meet you there." Jenna couldn't keep the smile off her face. The perfect summer was just one short road trip away.

"See ya. Bye, guys." Maureen poked her head in the backseat to make sure Nick and Ally had fastened their seat belts before clicking the car door closed.

All Jenna had to do before they were off was grab her purse and keys from the foyer.

"Bye, house," she said in a melodic voice as she locked the door.

Then, with a Beach Boys song playing in her head, she climbed behind the wheel and headed off for five weeks in paradise.

The island was less than an hour's drive from Savannah, but it might as well have been a world away. It was a sunny, sandy oasis, where Ally and Nick could play on the beach while Jenna worked on her manuscript without the pressures of homework, carpool and all the craziness that accompanied the school year. More importantly, it was their own special tradition—their first as a family of three.

Since her divorce four years ago, Jenna had sworn to herself that she'd still make Nick and Ally's childhoods as stable and happy as possible. According to her stack of parenting books, traditions instilled kids with comfort and a sense of belonging. The beach house rental had been their very first tradition as a trio. The summers Jenna spent at the beach as a kid were some of her fondest memories, so she'd booked a vacation home on Tybee the minute school was out. All these years later, it was still their favorite time of year.

Within minutes of merging onto the interstate, the lush oaks, cypresses and draping greenery of Savannah gave way to salty breezes and windswept marshes. When a seagull swooped into view, Jenna's heart gave a little squeeze. Every so often, she caught a glimpse of sand and cool blue ocean through a break in the vegetation.

Not much farther.

"How about a map update, Nick?" She met her son's gaze in the rearview mirror.

He peered at her cell phone, which she'd set to navigation and surrendered to the kids in hopes of avoiding the inevitable are-we-there-yet questions. "I think she just said we're close."

Ally moved to pry the phone out of his hands. "Is it near Ocean Burger?"

Nick shook his head and maintained his grip. "You always want to go to Ocean Burger."

"You always want to go to Splash Café," Ally countered.

True. Last summer Jenna could have run a shuttle bus between the two restaurants.

"Well, we're changing things up this year. New rental house, new summer camp." She and Maureen had found the perfect day camp for the kids, complete with beach activities and an Olympic-sized pool. While Ally was busy making sandcastles and Nick challenged Grayson to one freestyle race after another, Jenna would be free to work on her book in tranquil silence. It was a total win-win situation.

She just hoped the beach house she'd booked was as cozy and welcoming as it looked online. She'd been so consumed with working on the plot for her sequel that she'd booked their rental home later than usual. Consequently, the place they'd stayed for the past few years had been unavailable. She'd had no choice but to reserve someplace completely new. Luckily, she'd found something roomy enough, but the end of the school year had been crammed with so many activities that she hadn't even been able to do a drive-by and check it out.

"Does that mean it's not near Ocean Burger?" In the backseat, Ally deflated.

"We can still go. It just means that we have to drive to get there." Jenna glanced to her left, where the shore was beginning to stretch parallel to the highway, still barely visible through the sea oats. "All right, we're getting close. Tell me your goals."

Summer goal-setting was another of their family traditions. Last year, Nick caught his first fish in the surf and after days of combing through the sand, Ally accomplished her goal of finding a perfect, round sand dollar.

"I don't have anything new." Nick shrugged. "I just want to make swim team next year."

"You've got all summer to practice, bud. You can do it this time."

He was so close. Last year, he'd only missed the required lap time by ten seconds.

Ally's goal, on the other hand, was a

tad less serious. "Can I just eat chocolate all summer?"

Laughter bubbled up Jenna's throat. "Um, no. You can have *some* chocolate, but maybe you could pick a goal that's a little less...sugary?"

Ally thought for a minute. "Oh, I know! Play at camp so you can finish your book?"

Jenna nodded. "Both of our goals rolled into one. I like the efficiency."

"Thank you." Ally giggled, and Jenna had the distinct feeling that chocolate still had a prominent place on her daughter's summer agenda.

But right then, the beach came fully into view and goals suddenly seemed like the last thing Jenna should be worried about when so much beauty stretched out before them— the glittering blue ocean, sea oats dancing in the breeze and sand so white it made the shoreline look like an upturned bowl of sugar.

"Here it is! Are you guys excited? I'm excited!" Year after year, Jenna's first glimpse of the coast never failed to take her breath away. "You guys, check this out. The beach looks awesome."

Nick and Ally's backseat bickering gave way to happy chatter as she turned the car off the highway and onto Campbell Avenue at the intersection where the beach town's legendary welcome sign stood. *Welcome to Tybee Island!* Was it silly that the sight of that sign always made Jenna a little misty-eyed? Like the shore itself, the welcome sign with its giant sea turtle had been there as long as she could remember. The town's incorporation date, 1887, was proudly displayed beneath it. Tybee had been welcoming beachcombers for more than one hundred years, and in so many ways, coming here was like stepping back in time.

Life was simpler here...more peaceful.

And a peaceful summer was precisely what Jenna needed.

"Look at the turtle," Nick said.

Ally's reply was the same every year. "Oh, that's so cool."

Jenna smiled to herself and made a mental note to take the kids on a hunt for sea turtle nests on the dunes. Tybee was a nesting ground for endangered loggerhead turtles, and the island treated breeding loggerheads with great care.

"Oh, I can't wait." She took a deep breath and pulled into the short drive leading up to the beach house that would be their home for the next five weeks.

What if it wasn't as nice as it looked on the realty company's website? She'd splurged and used a good portion of her book advance to get a house right on the water. Jenna's first book had been an instant bestseller, allowing her to quit writing freelance articles for the Savannah Morning News. No more write-ups on local 5K fundraisers or lost dog notices. She was in the big leagues now. Sometimes this new career seemed too good to be true. Jenna just hoped that wasn't the case with the photos of the beach cottage she'd seen online. The pictures made the house seem so charming, so inviting.

Miraculously, the beach house stood at the end of the drive, looking even more idyllic in person than it had on the screen of her laptop. It was painted pale turquoise—the exact color of beach glass—with freshly painted white trim. The big shuttered windows promised a front-row seat to a summer of fiery ocean sunrises.

It was the perfect beach bungalow. And for five weeks, it was all theirs.

Sort of, anyway. Technically, since the house was a duplex, it was only *half* theirs. But half of this gorgeous place was all they needed.

Jenna let out a relieved exhale. "We're here."

Nick and Ally piled out of the car, too excited to remember their backpacks. Jenna grabbed her purse and caught up with them before they headed up the wooden staircase leading to the duplex's entrance. "All right you guys, let's check it out. We'll grab the stuff later."

"Man, this is awesome." Nick was the first to reach the top of the steps. He reached for the knob of the door to their half of the cottage. "This is us. Right here."

Ally bolted past him, toward the screened-in porch of their neighbor. "Dog! We've got a dog! I've always wanted one."

Oh, boy.

Jenna glanced over Ally's shoulder. Sure enough, a shaggy white dog sprawled belly-up on the cushion of their neighbor's white wicker sofa as if it was his own personal dog bed. "Not our dog, sweetie."

"Maybe like half of him is ours?" Ally was clearly taking the whole duplex concept a bit too far.

"Can we get the top half?" Nick said.

Probably the preferable half, if they were going to share the dog. Which they most definitely were *not*. "We don't even know if he's friendly yet."

Thankfully, Nick was more concerned about where he'd be sleeping than dividing up a strange dog. "I call top bunk."

Jenna was one step ahead of this argument. They'd been down this road four summers in a row. "Actually, we have two bunks."

Ally was still determined to one-up her brother. "Then I call biggest cookie."

Nick shook his head. "Do you ever stop thinking about food?"

"I don't know. Maybe someday when I'm older." Ally waved goodbye to the sleeping dog and followed Nick back to the proper half of the house so they could explore their summer home.

Jenna lingered for a moment. Her gaze shifted from the dog, all twitching paws and soft snores, to the surrounding mess. A damp wet suit was slung over a chair. The porch's floor was littered with sandy footprints, both human and canine, and dog toys. A half-empty coffee cup and what looked like a chunk of driftwood sat in the middle of a weathered coffee table. The table itself looked like something that might have washed up on the beach during a hurricane.

She inhaled a deep, yoga-esque breath.

The picture-perfect beach house she'd been dreaming about for weeks was, in fact, too good to be true. Her neighbor was a dog-owning slob. Were pets even legal in a short-term rental?

Don't panic.

In the scheme of things, it really wasn't a big deal, was it? Of course not. The mess wasn't Jenna's problem, even if the sight of the wetsuit activated her mothering instinct in a major way. If someone didn't hang it up soon, the chair's cushions would be soaked... which could lead to mold.

Again, not her problem.

She turned around and headed back to her own territory, nodding with satisfaction when she caught a glimpse of the screened-in porch on her half of the duplex—neat as a pin, complete with a stunning ocean view. Better yet, there wasn't a wet suit or strange animal in sight.

The inside of the cottage was just as charming as the exterior. Decorated in soft blues and greens, with sweeping sea views, it felt fit for a mermaid. She'd been silly to worry about the unseen neighbor.

"I think I can see the summer day camp from my bed," Nick said, as he and Ally sorted through a welcome basket the realty company had left on the whitewashed dining room table.

Jenna opened one of the bins they'd carried upstairs and peered inside. After a quick look at the house, they'd unloaded the car. All that was left to do was unpack. A place for everything and everything in its place. "It should be really close."

"Like walking-distance close?" Ally lifted a jar of Easter egg-hued candy from the basket and set it on the table.

"I think so," Jenna said.

The summer camp was situated right on

the beach with its own wooden deck leading to the smooth white sand and clear blue
water. Red and white bunting made it impossible to miss, as did the camp's cheery sign,
featuring a big yellow sun and swimmer and
surfboard graphics.

Beyond the waterfront deck and a beach
house that had been converted into the summer camp's headquarters, the camp spread
onto a vast back patio that boasted a competitive swimming pool and a tiki-style snack
bar. Jenna almost wished she could sign up
for day camp herself.

Ally grinned up at her, a bag of cookies
in each hand. "This welcome basket is really
cool."

Maybe Jenna should put her in charge of
a less sugar-centric chore.

"Why don't you guys tackle this box
while I take our beach toys out back?" She
nudged a plastic bin toward Ally and Nick,
then grabbed the crate containing their sand
shovels and buckets.

Just as she closed the door behind her,
she heard the kids' whispered exchange.

"I'll give you my cookies if you empty this
box," Nick said.

Ally's response was instantaneous and
enthusiastic. "Deal."

So much for keeping Ally away from
chocolate. It was okay, though. If Jenna's

biggest challenge this summer was taming her nine-year-old daughter's sweet tooth, the next five weeks would be every bit as blissful as she hoped.

Scratch that.

Jenna wasn't just hoping for a peaceful summer. If she wanted any chance at all of getting her book finished, she *needed* it. She needed it almost more than she wanted to admit.

Lucas McKinnon unzipped his wet suit, peeled it down to his waist and let the spray of the outdoor shower beat the salt and sand off his torso. If there was one thing he liked almost as much as a morning surf, it was a nice, hot shower afterward. The fact that the shower on the lower deck of the beach house offered him a clear, unobstructed view of the shore made it even sweeter.

The sea was unusually still today, as smooth and glassy as a mirror. Not so great for surfing, but undeniably pretty to look at it. Without the usual spray coming off the breakers, he could see the lighthouse looming in the distance. Just off the shore, a pair of dolphins crested the flat surface of the water, their silver forms glistening in the morning sunlight.

The calm before the storm.

Or so it seemed. In reality, the forecast was mild. Lucas checked the surf report every day like clockwork, and according to the TybeeWaves web site, there wouldn't be a raindrop in sight. Still, he couldn't remember the last time his little slice of the beach had been so serene. It was nearly as unsettling as it was beautiful.

Then just as he was about to flick the shower faucet to the off position, the stillness of the moment came to a colorful, bewildering close as a woman came bounding down the stairs.

"What the heck?" She gaped at him, wide-eyed and frozen in place.

For a minute, Lucas thought she might turn around and bolt back up the stairs.

"Whoa. Sorry, I'm sorry. I didn't expect a shower." Cheeks ablaze, she swallowed and averted her gaze. "Right in the middle of our place."

"Sorry about that." He gave the faucet a crank to the left and the shower's stream came to a dripping halt. "You must be the new neighbor."

The trickle of water slowed to a stop.

Plop.

Plop.

Plop.

Three slow drops, and she still couldn't bring herself to look at him.

"Um, yeah. We just checked in," she said to a nearby hibiscus bush, then nodded at the bin in her hands. "I just wanted to find somewhere to put this."

Wow, this was one jumpy woman. Lucas wasn't sure he'd ever seen a person who vibrated with such nervous energy. It rolled off of her in waves.

The forecast had been wrong. A storm had most definitely come to town. From the looks of things, a Category Four. Maybe even a Five.

"I don't think it really matters where you put it." He shrugged.

She glanced at him—cheeks flaring pink—and then quickly looked away again.

He grinned, trying to put her at ease. If she was going to react like this every time she saw someone in a bathing suit, she was in for an awfully long summer. "I'm Lucas, by the way. Lucas McKinnon."

"Well, Lucas. I'm going to let you finish what you're doing and I'm going to put this away." She held up the bin again, like it was some sort of protective barrier. "It was nice meeting you."

"Nice meeting you. Good luck." *Good luck unwinding enough to enjoy the beach.*

He watched as she strode past him, spine ramrod straight, until a ball of white fur came scampering down the stairs and leapt toward her.

"Oh, wow." She took a giant backward step.

Clearly not a dog person. Shocker.

"That's Tank." Lucas's rescue dog was probably the friendliest, most harmless creature on the island.

"Hi, Tank," she said as the pup pawed at her shins. Admittedly, Tank's greeting was a little exuberant, but surely she didn't think he'd actually harm her in any way. "Um, I should probably get inside before my kids think you ate me."

Kids? No wonder she seemed so tense.

"Get outta here, boy." Lucas pointed toward Tank's favorite shady spot in the sand.

The woman tiptoed a little dance and lifted her bin in the air as if Tank had a burning desire to devour her beach toys. "Down, down."

"Go," Lucas said, and Tank reluctantly scampered elsewhere.

Lucas cleared his throat. "So are those your kids I saw out front?"

"Last I checked, yeah." At last, she smiled at him.

It was a grin that knocked him unexpectedly off balance, as if he'd taken a tumble off his surfboard. "And your husband, is he...?"

She shook her head. "Ex-husband. He's in Japan for work."

"Oh." Now that they were face-to-face, he noticed what lovely eyes she had. They were a luminous amber, like an early morning sunrise glinting off the ocean. "You look kinda young to have kids that old."

"They're really not that old." She blinked. "But thank you? I think."

"And you don't have that caffeinated, dazed look that most parents have. You know the one where it's like they're just wrecked." Most parents he knew walked around like zombies, which was just one of the reasons Lucas had zero desire to join their ranks. "You know that kind?"

He pulled his best zombie face.

She lifted a brow. "So no kids for you, then?"

"Me? Oh, no. No, no, no." Just...*no.* "The furry kind are as close as I'm going to get to kids."

"Great." The expression on her face said otherwise. She was looking at him in much the same way she'd regarded Tank a few minutes ago. "Well, it was nice to meet you."

She'd already said it was nice meeting him, but somehow it sounded even less believable the second time around.

Lucas exchanged a glance with Tank as

she moved past him, heading toward the gate that led to the storage area under the stairs.

"We didn't," Lucas said to her back.

She turned around and propped the bin full of toys on her hip. Why did he get the feeling that her half of the duplex was currently filled with similar bins, all neatly packed and organized?

"I'm sorry?"

"We didn't officially meet," he said. "You never told me your name."

"Oh, right." She tilted her head, and her long, dark hair fell over her shoulder in glossy chestnut waves. Lucas wondered what she'd look like with beach hair, and then he wondered why he cared. "Jenna."

"Jenna," he echoed. "Jenna what?"

"Turner."

He shrugged. "Well, Jenna Turner. Now we've met."

"Yes, we have." She gave him a tight smile and reached for the latch on the gate. "Bye."

The latch didn't budge, and she fumbled furiously with it, storm clouds gathering in her eyes again.

He bit back a smile and mimed opening the latch. "You've got to push down on that."

She did as he indicated, and the gate swung open.

"Thanks." Her porcelain face bloomed

with color again and she darted through the gate, slamming the cottage door shut behind her.

Lucas couldn't help but laugh.

Category Five.

Most definitely.

Chapter Two

JENNA WAS A LITTLE RATTLED after her run-in with Lucas McKinnon.

Actually, she was *a lot* rattled.

But that was totally normal, right? It wasn't every day she ran into a strange man in the shower, even if said shower was located on the porch. The fact that he kept popping into her head as she unpacked boxes and got the beach house organized didn't necessarily mean anything.

Admittedly though, she was a tad curious about him. He'd acted so weird. Did he really think all parents were frazzled, dazed caffeine addicts?

She glanced at the coffee cup in her hand and set it down on the kitchen counter with a thunk. Without glancing in a mirror, she knew she probably looked a little bleary-eyed. She'd just moved her entire household into a new place for five weeks. Of course she was exhausted.

Too exhausted to write. And that was a problem.

But all she needed was a good night's sleep. Tomorrow the kids would be busy at summer camp, and she'd have the entire day to work. Shower Man didn't know what he was talking about. Just because she was a mom didn't mean she was a walking disaster. Ally and Nick were the best part of her life.

She yawned her way through the dazzling sunset, which was so spectacular that they decided to eat dinner on the picnic table on their upstairs deck. Afterward, the kids were just about as wiped out as Jenna was.

"Big day tomorrow, so let's try to sleep until the sun actually comes up." She stepped up the first few rungs of the ladder on Nick's bunk bed to give him a peck on the forehead.

"Tell that to Little Miss Chatty." Nick aimed a pointed glance at Ally.

Her bunk bed was adjacent to Nick's, and they'd both chosen to sleep up high. Ally pouted. "I happen to have a lot of important things to say."

"Yes, you do," Jenna said as her gaze snagged on the bright surfboard shaped cutouts that decorated the bed rails, yet another reminder of the surfer next door. "And we will talk about all of those things when the sun comes up. I love you monkeys."

This was going to be the perfect summer. The house was idyllic, despite her wet neighbor and his non-child-friendly vibe. She couldn't wait to get started on her book tomorrow. As soon as she got Ally and Nick off to camp, she'd take her laptop out to the deck and get an entire chapter knocked out.

Maybe even two.

But first, sleep.

She let out a long, luxurious sigh as she settled into the comfy king-sized bed in her new, temporary bedroom. But the second she closed her eyes, three loud barks traveled from one side of the duplex to the other.

Okay, so the walls were on the thin side. She'd just have to deal. It was just a little barking.

Except the barking was only the beginning, apparently.

"Tank. No barking," Lucas said in a voice loud enough for Jenna to hear every inflection.

She sat up straight. Did he realize the scolding was even more annoying than the barking itself?

Tank let out a few more yips, and Lucas corrected him again. "No barking."

This time, his voice was so crystal-clear that he might as well have been standing at the foot of her bed. Jenna plopped back down, and Lucas heaped effusive praise on the dog.

"Good boy!"

No, *not* good. Not good at all.

Was it too much to hope that she could finally get to sleep now that Tank had quieted down? Yes, apparently it was. Loud guitar music came streaming through the walls just as she closed her eyes again.

Jenna glanced at the clock on her nightstand. 11:13 p.m. "Seriously?"

Didn't Lucas McKinnon know what time it was? No wonder he didn't want kids. He *was* one.

Maybe she should go over there and ask him to turn the music down. But she was in her pajamas, and while they were a definite step up from a wet suit, she still didn't want to march over there in them. Her next conversation with Lucas needed to take place when they were both wearing actual clothes: shirts, shoes, the whole works. She'd feel ridiculous going over there in her PJs, and she was far too exhausted to climb into a pair of jeans and a t-shirt.

Besides, Nick and Ally didn't seem disturbed by the commotion. She was pretty sure she could hear Nick snoring across the hall.

Jenna buried her head under her pillow, but the rest of the night was more of the same. When her alarm went off the next morning, she was so tired she could barely drag herself out of bed to get the kids ready for camp. So much for getting a page or two written before making breakfast. At this rate, her word count might as well be a negative number.

The ride to summer camp was filled with animated chitchat. Nick and Ally had apparently gotten a great night's sleep, despite the rock concert that had gone on upstairs until the wee hours of the morning. Jenna squinted against the bright morning sunshine as she maneuvered the car into the camp parking lot, kicking herself for not confronting Lucas in the middle of the night. She felt like a zombie.

Maybe it was a good thing that Kayla, the head camp counselor, wore a whistle around her neck. Its piercing chirp kept Jenna from drifting off when she was supposed to be watching Nick's first freestyle lap.

How could she be dreaming of sleep when her son was so eager to dive right in? The camp's pool had three more lanes than the indoor pool where he swam during the school year in Savannah. Instead of a humid, stuffy natatorium, he was going to get to compete in the salty sea air, with seagulls and pelicans gliding overhead. The water glittered bright turquoise, and Jenna wished for what felt like the millionth time that she hadn't left her sunglasses in the car.

"There will be time trials at the beginning and end of the five weeks to track your progress," Kayla said as the kids lined up at the pool's edge. "Think of it as your personal best. Aside from that, summer camp is all about having fun!"

Jenna smiled, despite her exhaustion. *Fun* was precisely why she'd enrolled Nick and Ally in camp, and with her flippy blonde hair and bubbly persona, Kayla definitely seemed capable of making that happen.

Nick was already grinning ear-to-ear. He pulled his swim goggles over his head and glanced at Grayson, standing first in line at the lane beside him. "You want to race to the end?"

Grayson struck his best Michael Phelps pose. "To the end and back."

Seated beside Jenna on the bleachers, Maureen shook her head. "Let me guess—they're already competing?"

"It never fails with these two," Jenna said.

"So what do you say, are we ready to get this party started?" Kayla's whistle sounded, followed by the splash of dozens of kids cannonballing into the water.

Still, Jenna could barely keep her eyes open.

"It looks like Nick is really pushing himself." Maureen's eyebrows rose as she watched the boys make their way across the pool.

"He is. He just needs a little more self-confidence, that's all."

Maureen's gaze shifted toward Jenna. "And it looks like you need a little more sleep."

She sighed. "I blame my neighbor for that."

"Why does that sound more scandalous than it is?"

As if. Never in a million years.

"He blasted music all night. Who does that?" Jenna pulled a face.

"Isn't he a surfer?"

Like that explained anything. Or made her complete and total sleep deprivation okay. The only thing that could make it all better was a nap, plus maybe a Tylenol for her splitting headache.

"Yeah, a messy one who probably sleeps until ten every day," Jenna said.

She couldn't fathom the luxury of staying in bed so late. Not that she wanted to, exactly. She had things to do, pancakes to make, and a book to write. Still, it would have been nice if sleeping in was even an option. Jenna couldn't remember the last time her bed hadn't already been neatly made before six-thirty in the morning.

Maureen shrugged. "What do I always tell my students?"

"Middle school is like Middle-earth?" Maureen had always had a not-so-secret Hobbit obsession.

"That." Maureen nodded. "*And* you should always follow the two-week rule."

She shot Jenna a meaningful glance.

Jenna wasn't altogether sure what she was talking about, but she had a feeling it had something to do with her music-loving neighbor. And since she didn't want to think about Lucas McKinnon, much less talk about him, she turned her attention back to the pool where Nick and Grayson were swimming alongside one another, neck-and-neck.

"Looking good, Nick," Jenna called. But she could still feel Maureen's gaze on her, so she finally relented. "What's the two-week rule?"

"You should always give it that long before you decide if you like someone or not. I mean, otherwise, it's a snap judgment."

She had a point, but Jenna wasn't a kid in middle school. She was a grown-up, unlike a certain surfing enthusiast who lived right on the other side of her paper-thin walls.

Besides, Jenna didn't judge people. That was wrong. "Yeah, I don't do that."

"Really?"

"Mm-hmm."

Maureen lifted a brow. "What about Mr. Splenda?"

Jenna had totally forgotten about him. They'd gone out on exactly one date, during which Mr. Splenda emptied five yellow packets onto his salad. *His salad!* "Okay, he had a seriously unhealthy addiction to sweetener."

Maureen stifled a grin. "And Airplane Guy?"

"He took his shoes and socks off before we were airborne." Yuck. "Besides, that was a dating thing...."

"Which you can't keep avoiding."

"I'm not avoiding it. I'm just approaching it with a much more critical eye this time around." She had to. Hers wasn't the only heart at stake anymore. She had Nick and Ally to think about now.

"That sounds so romantic." Maureen fluttered her eyelashes mockingly.

Why on earth was she going down that road?

"Either way, this is a neighbor thing." *Not* a romance thing, even though Jenna wondered if she was being slightly unfair to Lucas. She didn't want to be the kind of person who judged people, and after all, it had only been one night. Maybe the loud music was the exception rather than the rule.

Then again, maybe it wasn't. She'd been right on the other side of the wall. He had to have known she'd hear it. "And trust me, he's totally Mr. Slack."

Maureen gave Jenna one of her teacher stares—the kind that never failed to make her middle school students admit the dog hadn't actually eaten their homework.

And just like an eighth grader, Jenna folded beneath the weight of the teacher stare. "Okay, fine. I'll give it two weeks."

Isn't that what she'd tell her kids to do? Yes, it was.

She glanced at Ally, splashing around the shallow end of the pool with a group of girls who looked to be about her age. Making friends already...probably because she always gave new people a chance.

Maureen nodded. "Good."

Good.

Jenna just hoped that the next fourteen days weren't anything like the past twenty-four hours. Otherwise she'd never get her book finished.

The next morning, Jenna got Nick and Ally off to summer camp and returned to the beach house ready to work. She set her laptop in the center of the picnic table on the deck, along with a cup of coffee, her hardback thesaurus, and yes, her trusty antique typewriter. Desperate times called for desperate measures. She didn't actually use it much for typing, but she'd inherited it from her grandfather, who'd written four books on the clunky old thing—cowboy stories in the vein of Zane Grey and Louis L'Amour. Since he'd definitely managed to avoid the one-hit-wonder problem back in his day, she considered his typewriter her good luck charm.

Jenna took a deep inhale of salty sea air. She could do this. The few pages she'd managed to write before the summer move to the beach house were printed out and held in place with a giant conch shell. Her deck sat just behind the dune, affording her a perfect view of the gently tumbling ocean. Early morning sun glittered on the water, and there wasn't a soul on the beach this early in the day. She couldn't have asked for a more tranquil writing environment.

Time to get to work.

She took a generous sip of coffee and began flipping through the manuscript. The story was in better shape than she'd thought, thank goodness. She just needed to incorporate the changes she'd marked in the margins with red pencil, and then she could start writing the second half.

But as soon as she opened her laptop, a

familiar streak of white leapt onto the table. "What the...?"

Tank!

The dog's wagging tail sent the conch shell flying and Jenna barely had time to slam her hand down on top of her pages to protect them from the wind. "No, no, no, Tank."

He pawed at her hand, clearly thinking they were playing some kind of game. Then he went for the coffee cup as if it were a dog bowl.

Please, no. The last thing he needed was caffeine. "Aw, come on, man."

He looked up to give her a puppy kiss, knocking the coffee over in the process. Dark liquid poured over her pages. "Not the book!"

Her notes were fading before her eyes. Now she was going to have to re-read everything and start the editing process all over again. So much for spending the afternoon plotting out new material.

Jenna looped a finger beneath Tank's collar and helped him hop off the table. "Let's go. Time to go home."

She guided the dog down the white wooden staircase toward Lucas's front door and as luck would have it, he stepped outside just as she and Tank reached the bottom step.

His porch was every bit as messy as the

last time Jenna had seen it. Half-empty bottles of water were scattered about, and the swing was littered with surf magazines. While he'd somehow managed to hang his wet suit on a hook, a damp towel lay piled into one of the chairs.

Jenna bit back the mildew lecture she gave her kids every time she found a towel on the bathroom floor.

"Hey." He gave her a lopsided grin, which made Jenna feel like he might actually be happy to see her.

Odd...

And completely irrelevant.

"Hey." She glanced down at Tank, wagging his tail in glee. "I think this guy belongs to you."

Honestly, hadn't Mr. Slack ever heard of leash laws?

The dog was awfully cute, though. Maybe he was just trying to run away from the loud music and general chaos of Lucas's side of the house. Jenna couldn't really blame him.

Lucas's expression went all ooey-gooey at the sight of his canine bestie, and he picked up his usual laid-back pace. "Whatcha doing over there? Get in here, you." He pushed the screen door open. "Get in."

Jenna released her hold on Tank's collar and he trotted past Lucas to pounce on one of the dog toys strewn on the worn wooden floor of the porch.

"Either trying to play with, or rearrange, my book. I don't know. It's really hard to say." Jenna forced a smile. As adorable as Tank was, she still had coffee-stained pages to contend with on the upstairs deck.

Lucas shot her another of his boyish grins. "Well, I always said he'd make a great editor."

She might have even considered Lucas and his scruffy little mutt charming if they weren't so wholly annoying.

"No?" He leaned against the doorjamb and shrugged one shoulder.

"No. Cute, but no." Now wasn't the time to give in, no matter how sweet the surfer and his doggy bestie were together. "Hey, one other quick thing, if you have a second."

"Yeah, of course. Come on in." He held the screen door open for her and motioned for Tank to follow when they reached the entry to the duplex. "Come on, buddy. Inside."

Lucas's half of the house was a mirror image of Jenna's, decorated in the same calming beach glass hues. A strand of colorful lights lined the walls of the living room and a bright blue electric guitar sat propped in a corner. *The* guitar, no doubt.

Other than a table piled with books and a basket of clean, unfolded laundry, the space was remarkably tidy. Wonders never ceased.

Remember the two-week rule.

She pasted on her best neighborly smile. "So, I just wanted to ask or maybe suggest we set some ground rules."

Lucas grabbed a plastic bin of dog food from the kitchen counter and began to scoop kibble into a metal bowl. "Yeah? About what?"

Tank trotted past her, tags jangling. "Well, the dog, for starters."

"Oh." Lucas flipped the plastic bin closed and set Tank's bowl on the floor. "You're not a dog person."

"No, I love dogs." She just didn't love it when they jumped all over her manuscript and interrupted a rare moment when she was getting some actual work done. That hadn't been Tank's fault, of course. She blamed Lucas. No wonder he didn't have kids. If he did, he'd probably lose track of them in a heartbeat. "I mean, I like them, my daughter loves them, and my ex-husband keeps promising to get them one, but I'm just too busy to commit to a dog right now. I mean it wouldn't be fair to the little guy. Especially considering I have this book deadline and I'm not quite sure how I'm going to hit it."

Stop. Talking.

She couldn't seem to stop the flow of

nonsense coming out of her mouth. Why was she rambling? Moreover, what was it about Lucas that made her so nervous?

He didn't need to know what she did for a living. They weren't friends. They were neighbors—*temporary* neighbors.

"Oh, you're a writer?" Lucas looked up from the dishtowels he'd begun folding sometime during her monologue. "What do you write? Like, novels or plays?"

"Teen fiction," Jenna said.

He gave her a blank look.

Oh, no. She'd seen that look before—on her ex-husband's face. As amicable as their split had been, he wasn't exactly supportive of her career as an author. Never had been. When they'd been married, he never really understood why she stayed up late to write after the kids had gone to bed. The way he'd seen it, she'd been wasting her time on a book for teenagers when she already had a job writing about community events for the local paper. Even after she'd signed with an agent and accepted a publishing deal, he'd been happy for her but unconvinced. After all, one book didn't make a career.

Sometimes she wondered if he was right. Could she really do this?

"It's a lot harder than it sounds," she added. "Which is why I can't risk any distractions right now. So, I was hoping you could keep Tank on your side of the fence, so to speak."

He laughed as if she'd just asked the impossible. "Sorry. I can't do that."

Not exactly the reaction she was expecting. In fact, it was the exact opposite. "What?"

"There *is* no fence. It's a shared patio."

"But you know what I mean." Observing the two-week rule was getting tougher by the second. "Also, I don't know if you realize, but the walls are like, paper-thin. So if you could keep the music down past, let's say—"

"Look, Jenna," he said, cutting her off as he moved from folding towels to refilling the coffee pot. Was he even listening to her at all? "I really appreciate you bringing Tank back, but I live here year-round."

"Right." He had to be joking. The living room was nice, but completely lacking family photos or any of the ordinary personal touches that made a house a home. "You don't even have any plants."

"What does that have to do with anything?"

Spoken like a true bachelor. No kids, no plants. Nothing at all that required nurturing.

"Never mind." She took a deep breath. "You were saying?"

He put the coffee pot back in its cradle

and gave her his full attention. Finally. "I get that you're going to be here for a month..."

"It's five weeks, actually." Not that she expected him to adhere to any sort of calendar. The tide charts were probably as close as he got to a proper schedule.

"Right." That oh-so-charming smile of his was beginning to get on her nerves. "Either way, I'll do my best. But you might just want to learn how to relax."

Jenna's mouth dropped open. He did *not* just say that. "I'm sorry? You want me to... to relax?"

"Yeah." He shrugged as if he hadn't just insulted her right to her face. "I mean, it might be good for you."

She crossed her arms and stared at him.

"Just as a suggestion," he said. After an awkward pause, he added, "Anything else?"

So. Much. Else.

She could have waxed poetic about how obnoxious he'd been during the past five minutes alone, but she didn't want to stand there and argue with him anymore. Because, hello, she had a book to write! "Nope. I think we're all set."

He nodded, and she spun on her heel to go. The last thing she heard before she shut the door behind her was Lucas showering Tank with praise for finishing his dinner.

"Good boy," he gushed.

Her heart gave a little tug, but she refused to fall for the lovable pet-parent act. Cute could only go so far.

"Relax? You want me to relax?" she muttered to herself as she stomped back upstairs. "Please. I'm *totally* relaxed."

She looked down at the charming little picnic table, now in a state of total disarray. Her coffee cup lay on its side and the damp pages of her manuscript were scattered out of order. The conch shell could barely keep the mess pinned under control.

Jenna fumed, grabbing her cell phone from atop the thesaurus. She couldn't let Lucas get to her. He had no clue what kind of pressure she was under and trying to explain it to him was getting her nowhere. It was time to do something drastic so she didn't end up as a literary one-hit wonder. She scrolled through the contacts on her phone, thumb moving furiously over the little screen until she landed on Maureen's number.

Her friend answered on the first ring. "Hey!"

"Hey." The ocean roared behind her. Even the waves seemed stirred up after her encounter with Lucas. "So forget this two-week rule. I need your help."

Mr. Slack thought she needed to relax, did he?

Relaxing wouldn't help matters when

it came to dealing with someone like Lucas McKinnon, but Jenna knew precisely what would.

Chapter Three

TECHNICALLY, JENNA NEEDED HELP FROM Maureen's husband rather than Maureen herself. Ian was one of Savannah's most sought-after contractors, so handling a project like the one she had in mind would probably be a piece of cake. But convincing him to pick up a hammer on his vacation would probably be easier with Maureen on board.

Whatever Maureen said to Ian must have worked because he showed up the following afternoon with his tools and a truck full of wood from the island's hardware store. If Jenna wasn't mistaken, he even seemed a little excited about giving his toolbox a workout. She and Maureen tried to help, but Ian insisted on doing the bulk of the work himself.

In two short hours, he was nearly finished. He tucked a pencil behind his ear and stepped back to inspect his handiwork, crossing his arms over his broad chest. Ian had the solid build of a man who spent most of his time working with his hands. In his deck shoes and beach khakis, he looked ready to construct a boat dock or a fishing pier.

"I think this should do it." Ian nodded toward the newly constructed fence she'd hired him to build. It was a darling white picket barrier that stretched from one end of the duplex's deck to the other, neatly dividing the space in two. Better yet, Ian had managed to design it so that it stood completely on its own, so Jenna wouldn't need to bother the beach house's rental company for permission. At the end of the summer, she could just take it apart and move on.

Yes, it was a rather drastic solution to the Tank problem. But Lucas hadn't given her a choice, had he? He'd refused to even entertain the notion of keeping Tank out of her space. He'd told her to *relax*, as if he knew anything about her at all.

Well, he didn't. And he wouldn't because now she could stay on her side of the fence, and he could keep his mess and his dog and his superior attitude on the other side.

Maureen planted her hands on her hips. "If I had my way, I'd lock you two in detention until you worked it out."

Jenna shot her a knowing look. "But

there's nothing to work out because I called it."

Maureen's gaze narrowed. "So he really is Mr. Slack?"

"And completely arrogant, which is a deadly combo," Jenna said.

Ian pointed at the fence with his hammer. "I thought you said this fence was for the dog."

"It is." Of course it was. The fact that the fence would keep Lucas away too was just a bonus. Plus, it was only four feet high—a perfectly normal, dog-sized fence. "It totally is."

Ian stifled a laugh and Maureen just shook her head.

Whose side were they on, anyway? "Come on, don't act like I'm the unreasonable one."

Maureen's gaze swiveled from Jenna to the fence and back again. "I just think it's a little extreme."

"Or an easy solution." Why did Jenna sound so unsure all of a sudden? And why did a little ball of guilt seem to be curling up in the pit of her stomach? The fence had seemed like a great idea twenty-four hours ago when she'd called Maureen and Ian.

Besides, it was a little late to be having second thoughts.

"All right." Ian nodded. "Now listen, unless you want me to start building a moat, this is as far as I can go."

"A moat, see, that would be extreme." Lucas would probably just surf right across it, anyway.

Speak of the devil.

The door to Lucas's half of the house swung open and out he came, all lean muscle and easy charm. With his damp hair, flip-flops, and ocean-blue shirt, he looked as chill and perfect as a model in a J. Crew catalog. Jenna's heart fluttered ever so slightly, which she chalked up to nerves over the fence situation.

"Oh, hey." She swallowed.

Lucas carried a frosty glass of iced tea in his hand, which paused halfway to his mouth when he spotted the fence.

His stared hard at the crisp white wood. "Wow, that was fast."

"So, you got my note?" Jenna gestured toward the fence, which was beginning to feel more like a line drawn in the sand. "About all this?"

"I got it. I just didn't think anyone moved that quickly. On anything." He rested a hand on top of one of the pointed fenceposts and peered at her from the other side. Why did it seem like every time he met her gaze her pulse kicked up a notch? "Especially a fence."

"It helps to know a contractor." Jenna smiled and tipped her head toward Ian.

Maureen aimed a playful grimace at her husband. "I thought it would help to marry one, but I'm still waiting on my new porch."

"That's because I've been so fixated on you," Ian said.

Maureen shook her head. "You're lying, but at least it sounds cute when you're smiling."

Jenna's own marriage had been nothing like Maureen and Ian's. Sometimes they were so adorable together that it hurt to look at them. Especially now, while Lucas McKinnon stood on his side of the patio looking at her like she'd lost her mind.

"Oh, sorry." Jenna realized she should probably make introductions. Not that the four of them would be hanging out together any time soon. Or ever. "Lucas, this is Maureen and Ian. My good friends from home. Guys, this is Lucas."

They exchanged hellos and shook hands over the top of the fence.

"We've heard so much about you," Maureen said.

Really? She made it sound like Jenna had been talking about Lucas nonstop. And thinking about him too, which she most definitely hadn't.

Keep telling yourself that.

"All good, of course," Maureen added.

"Now *you're* lying." Lucas sipped his tea.

They'd officially ventured into awkward territory. Maureen shifted her gaze to Ian. "Should we go?"

Ian wasted zero time grabbing his toolbox. "I think we should go."

"Thank you. I appreciate it. See you guys." Jenna waved as they headed down the deck's staircase.

Once Ian and Maureen were out of sight, Jenna turned to find Lucas watching her with unabashed amusement. How had she never noticed the dimple in his left cheek?

Her face went hot. "Just so you know, the fence is for Tank. To help me 'relax,' as you so poetically put it." She made little air quotes around the word *relax* because she just couldn't resist.

Lucas took another long, lazy sip of tea before responding. "Sure it is."

"What's that supposed to mean?"

He said nothing. He just kept looking at her like he could see straight inside her head, and then the corner of his mouth hitched into a smug half-grin as he started to walk away.

Good. Didn't he have a wave to ride somewhere?

But before he could take more than a

step, Nick and Ally came bounding down the outdoor stairs from the house's upper deck.

"Don't go too far. Stay where I can see you," Jenna said as they ran past her, headed toward the beach.

"Okay, Mom," Ally called over her shoulder.

"Have fun!" Jenna crossed her arms and watched to make sure they didn't get too close to the water. "Be safe but have fun."

Ally tossed a frisbee to Nick as they crested the dune and he caught it just before it plowed into the sand.

Beside her, Lucas nodded. "I'm just saying I get it."

Why was he still standing there?

"Get what?" she asked before she could stop herself.

"I get it. I'll keep my furry kid on this side, if you keep your kids on..." He pointed to the space opposite his portion of the patio. "That side."

"Oh, you want me to keep my kids contained?" Of course he did. Why was she the slightest bit surprised?

"It only seems fair." He shrugged and ambled back toward the door to his half of the house. "Doesn't it?"

She pasted on a smile. "All right. Fine."

And to think she'd actually felt guilty when he'd first walked outside and spotted the fence. His easy smile had vanished the second he'd set eyes on it. Jenna hated to be the source of such a crestfallen expression, and her first thought had been that she'd taken their war of words too far by putting an actual, physical barrier between them. She'd also been somewhat worried that she'd hurt his feelings somehow, despite his refusal to cooperate with her—at all.

What had she been thinking? She had zero reason to feel guilty. The fence was the perfect solution. Lucas McKinnon was impossible. Jenna couldn't deal with him for five straight weeks, and now she wouldn't have to.

Out of sight, out of mind.

She took a deep inhale of salty sea air and smiled at the white picket masterpiece. "I feel better already."

Lucas wasn't sure why he was letting his odd neighbor get under his skin. Ordinarily, he had no trouble going with the flow and minding his own business. He was a peaceful person. And Jenna wasn't the first uptight, big-city type to rent the other half of the beach house.

But she was definitely the first to construct a fence straight down the middle of the deck.

Who did that?

He couldn't seem to shake off the question. How could he, when every time he looked out the window, he caught a glimpse of that ridiculous white-picket monstrosity?

He'd almost let himself believe that Jenna would come to her senses and tear the thing down before the sun came up the next morning, but no. It was still there when he and Tank wandered outside to watch the sun rise over the ocean, bathing the sea in soft pinks and yellows.

Too bad the water was so calm. What Lucas really needed was a good surf, but that wasn't going to happen. Instead, he grabbed a couple of sawhorses from his storage shed and propped one of his boards on top of them. He'd have to work off his irritation with a piece of sandpaper instead of riding a wave.

He sanded the surfboard in smooth, circular motions while Tank watched from a nearby deck chair. The tension in Lucas's shoulders eased almost at once, and he couldn't help smiling as Tank's scruffy little head swiveled back and forth, following his movements.

Then two other small heads popped up from the other side of the new fence, Nick and Ally. And just like that, Lucas's shoulders stiffened again.

Don't engage.

Lucas wasn't a family man. He wouldn't know how to be one, even if he tried. His father hadn't exactly been the best role model in that department. He'd spent more time at the office than he had at home when Lucas was growing up, right up until the day he had a fatal heart attack while sitting at his desk.

After business school, when Lucas found himself falling into the same workaholic trap, he'd gotten out while he still could. Life was a gift—one that shouldn't be wasted. So, he'd headed to Tybee and never looked back. His life was simple now. Uncomplicated.

Just the way he liked it.

He focused intently on his board. He didn't even make eye contact with either of Jenna's kids, but they didn't seem to take the hint.

"How often do you walk him?" Ally said.

Lucas looked up and found her staring longingly at Tank.

The dog was usually more into snoring than walking. Lucas shrugged. "I don't know. He's kind of low-maintenance."

"Because I could do it if you want." The girl bobbed up and down, brimming with excess energy.

Did kids always get up this early? It was summer. Shouldn't they be sleeping in?

"I think we're good," Lucas said.

"Or I could teach him how to sit. Or roll over."

Tank learning new tricks was about as likely as Jenna learning how to relax. *Not going to happen.* Ally called out to Tank, peppering him with orders. The dog's eyes drifted closed.

"I bet you're a really good swimmer, right?" Nick grinned over the top of the fence. "Since you surf all the time."

Great. Now the little boy was chiming in. Wasn't the new construction supposed to stop this sort of interaction?

Lucas shrugged. "I wasn't always."

"But you are now?" The boy's face scrunched up, which emphasized the light sprinkling of freckles across the bridge of his nose.

Cute kid, Lucas thought. Or he might have thought so if he were a kid person. "Are you guys always this chatty in the morning?"

"Not me. She's the early riser." Nick tipped his head toward his sister.

She grinned and pointed double finger guns at Tank. "Which is why I can walk your dog."

As if on cue, Tank yawned.

Lucas stifled a smile. "He likes to sleep in while I'm surfing."

"Do you think you could give me some pointers?" Nick's eyes brimmed with hope.

Lucas narrowed his gaze. "On surfing?" Nick's mom would just love that, wouldn't she?

"Just swimming," he said. The metal retainer on his bottom teeth reminded Lucas of his own awkward middle school years. "I need to cut my time to make swim team next year."

Nostalgia aside, Lucas's response was automatic. "You know, I'm not much of a teacher."

Nick wasn't giving up. "Even if—"

"Sorry," Lucas said, cutting him off. He didn't want to give the kid even a whiff of false hope. "It's really not my thing, buddy."

Lucas had no interest in trying to be a role model for Jenna Turner's precious children. One wrong step and he'd never hear the end of it. She already seemed to think his lack of houseplants meant he was some kind of deadbeat. Since when had ferns become a hallmark of responsibility?

Besides, dogs were much easier than kids. Dogs were sweet. Dogs were loyal. They loved naps and didn't mind eating the same food every day. They didn't require help with their homework or braces for their teeth or a college education.

Best of all, dogs loved with their whole hearts. Lucas didn't have to worry about letting Tank down. His dog had never once looked at him with anything other than complete adoration in his soft, brown eyes.

Kids, on the other hand, were far more complicated.

And if the crushed expression on Jenna's son's face was any indication, they were also much easier to disappoint.

What a difference a day makes.

Or more accurately, a fence.

Jenna stood at the pretty turquoise stove in her half of the beach house and flipped a pancake over with a flick of the spatula. Two place settings of beachy pastel china were already set out on the kitchen counter, along with a pitcher of fresh orange juice and warm maple syrup.

She was in a far better mood this morning than the previous one. She hadn't heard a peep from the other side of the duplex since the discussion surrounding the fence. No loud guitar music, no barking, no Lucas.

It was bliss.

She'd slept like a baby and even managed to wake up early enough to write two full pages before getting Nick and Ally out of bed. Boom. Meanwhile, Mr. Slack would probably roll out of bed at noon.

Fine. He could do whatever he wanted over there across the fence. Jenna didn't care one way or another. She had a book to write and pancakes to make. Since she was in such a celebratory mood, she'd tossed a generous portion of chocolate chips into the batter. Ally would be thrilled.

Jenna called upstairs, ready for a stampede. "Who wants the first stack of pancakes?"

Her kids considered pretty much everything a competition, so she figured they'd be barreling down the stairs within seconds. But when she glanced at the ceiling, bracing for impact, there was no response whatsoever.

She tried again. "Nick? Ally?"

Still nothing from inside the house, but a few familiar yips drifted through the open window.

Tank, of course. But why was he barking all of a sudden, just when Nick and Ally had gone conspicuously missing?

Oh no.

Jenna dropped the spatula as Lucas's words rang in her head, clear as a bell.

I'll keep my furry kid on this side if you keep your kids on that side.

She couldn't be the one to break their delicate truce. Not after he'd looked at her like she was a crazy person for dividing the deck into halves. If Ally and Nick were on the other side of the fence, he'd never let her live it down. It would be humiliating—*beyond* humiliating—and she wasn't sure she could take five straight weeks of looking at Lucas's smug surfer grin.

Even if that grin was framed by a set of oh-so-appealing dimples.

She blinked. What was she thinking? She couldn't possibly find Lucas McKinnon attractive. There was nothing nice about him whatsoever. Not his sandy wetsuit that he constantly left lying around, not his surfboards that were strewn all over the patio, and not his late-night guitar music. Not even his dimples.

Or the goofy voice he used when he talked to his scruffy little dog.

Okay, maybe that last one was kind of dreamy. But that didn't mean she was attracted to him. It didn't even mean she liked him.

Yip.

Tank barked again, snapping her back to reality. What was she doing? Why was she standing around reminding herself of all the reasons she disliked Lucas when the pancakes were getting cold?

Something was definitely happening outside on the deck. She needed to find Nick and Ally.

Now.

Lucas had been sanding his surfboard for nearly fifteen minutes, but it wasn't any smoother than when he'd started. There were exactly two reasons for his staggering lack of progress, and those reasons were named Nick and Ally.

They were still interrogating him—about swimming, surfing, dogs and an assortment of other random subjects that popped into their heads. Lucas couldn't help admiring their persistence. He'd thought they would've given up by now, seeing as he wasn't exactly encouraging the interaction.

They didn't seem to notice, though. Their arms were draped over the fence, inching them higher so they wouldn't miss a thing happening on his side of the patio.

Surprisingly, Lucas didn't mind. Much.

Tank, however, was another story. The poor dog was still being ordered about by Ally.

Sit. Lie down. Roll over. Speak.

Her list of demands was vast. But Tank being Tank, he refused to budge from his comfy spot on the deck chair. Other than an occasional yip of protest, Ally's commands were falling on deaf ears.

"I think something is wrong with him." She tilted her head. "He won't sit. Or listen."

Lucas glanced at Tank. The pup's eyelids were getting heavy. Any minute now he'd be chasing beach balls in his dreams.

Lucas's gaze shifted back to Ally. "He likes to move at his own pace."

"Kind of like his owner." The singsong lilt in Ally's tone told Lucas she was repeating an opinion she'd heard elsewhere. From her mother, most likely.

Lucas sighed. "Don't you guys have to get ready for camp or something?"

The second the words left his mouth, Jenna appeared at the foot of the staircase. "They do."

Her windswept hair was gathered to one side, and a coffee cup was cradled in her hands. She wore a denim shirt over a plain white tee with cherry-red jeans. For some reason, the unexpected pop of color made Lucas smile, and he couldn't help but wonder what she'd been doing upstairs for the past half hour. She looked—dare he think it—relaxed.

Almost.

She cleared her throat. "Which is why they should be upstairs getting ready instead of down here bothering you."

Lucas leaned closer to Nick and Ally. "Her words, not mine."

He'd never said they were bothering him. They seemed like good kids, although Tank might disagree.

Jenna shot him a disbelieving glance over the rim of her coffee cup.

"But what if we're already ready?" Nick said. Neither he nor Ally budged.

"Does that mean you don't want your pancakes?" Jenna asked. So that's what she'd been doing up there. Making pancakes. "Because I'm sure Tank would love to eat them."

A joke! Lucas could hardly believe it. He volleyed one back to her. "He prefers small children."

Nick and Ally's eyes went as wide as saucers.

Seriously? Tank was as gentle as they came. "I'm kidding."

"Cute," Jenna said without a hint of sarcasm. She sounded as if she might actually mean it.

Lucas felt himself smiling. They were actually being civil to one another. They might even be flirting.

No way. Not possible. His smile faded on his lips. *Was it?*

"Did you put chocolate chips in them?" Ally said.

Right...the pancakes. Breakfast sounded nice. Jenna was probably the type of mom who used pretty cloth napkins and warmed up the syrup. Lucas's stomach rumbled, and he hoped no one heard it.

Jenna swept a lock of hair behind her

ear. She was getting closer and closer to beach hair every day. "I might have."

The promise of a chocolate-laden breakfast was all it took to tear the kids away from the fence. Finally.

"Yes!" Ally bolted for the stairs.

Nick wasn't far behind.

"I'll meet you up there," Jenna said as they whizzed past her.

Then it was just the two of them, and Lucas suddenly found himself short of breath.

Relaxation suits her.

Not that he had any business making such an observation when she'd constructed a literal barrier to keep him away.

Still, she lingered at the foot of the stairs for a minute as if she wanted to say something. He couldn't imagine what it might be.

She took a deep breath. "Well, have a nice day."

Lucas nodded. "I always do."

How could he not have a great day when he lived in the most beautiful spot on earth and wasn't bogged down by a house full of potted plants?

He laughed quietly to himself until he realized he was watching Jenna climb back up the stairs. He didn't envy her position as a single parent, but she made it look almost effortless. And he had to admire her work ethic and dedication to her writing. Plus there was

a hint of amber in her brown eyes that reminded him of summer sunsets and skies
ablaze with golden light. He loved those eyes,
even when they were regarding him with cool
indifference.

When he averted his gaze, he found Tank
regarding him with keen interest. The dog
cocked his head and let out a soft woof.

Lucas's gaze narrowed. "What are you
thinking, boy?"

Was Tank contemplating how long he
could avoid Ally's enthusiastic brand of dog
training? Was he wondering what Jenna had
wanted to tell him before she'd retreated back
upstairs? Or was he simply thinking about
pancakes?

Probably the latter, but Lucas liked to
think it might be all of the above.

"Me, too."

Chapter Four

NICK'S REQUEST FOR HELP WITH his swim lessons had nothing to do with Lucas's decision to stop by the summer camp for lunch a few days later. Zero. He had every right to be there, and it wasn't as if he'd never dropped by before.

After all, he owned the place.

Contrary to whatever Jenna Turner believed, Lucas wasn't a worthless beach bum. Sure, he liked to surf. And admittedly, his daily schedule wasn't always set in stone. But that didn't necessarily mean he didn't work for a living. He just typically took a more hands-off approach where the summer camp was concerned. Kayla was the best employee he'd ever had. Every summer for the past three years, she'd had the camp running like clockwork.

Still. He decided it wouldn't hurt to pop in and check on things.

The wooden planks of the deck creaked

beneath his feet as he made his way from the shore to the summer camp entrance. As usual, the railing was lined with campers' colorful beach towels, left out to dry in the sun. The bright rows of flags strung overhead flapped in the cool ocean breeze.

As fate would have it, he got there just as Nick was nearing the end of a lap in the pool. At least Lucas told himself it was fate, because he still wasn't quite ready to accept that he was seriously thinking about helping the kid.

He hung back by the bleachers and watched as Nick made a slow crawl to the end of his lane. All the other kids were already out of the water and peeling off their goggles by the time Nick grabbed onto the concrete edge of the pool, panting for breath.

Kayla blew her whistle. "Good job, guys. Let's break for lunch."

The campers hustled toward the picnic tables, barely managing to follow the pool's *no running* rule. Kayla kept an eye on them and waited for Nick to drag himself out of the cool blue water.

"Come on, dude. Those fish tacos are calling your name." She gave him a playful tap as he stood dripping on the deck.

Shoulders slumped and eyes downcast, he clearly wasn't in any hurry to get something to eat. "I'm not really that hungry."

Inwardly, Lucas winced. The kid must be really upset if a fish taco couldn't pull him out of his funk. They were the camp specialty.

Kayla shot him a sympathetic grin. "I can't have anyone passing out on my watch, so you're gonna have to eat something."

Nick sighed. He looked so small out there, so vulnerable. His shark-pattered swimsuit hung all the way down to his knees.

A strange ache churned in the pit of Lucas's stomach. He'd been that kid once, and it hadn't been fun.

"I promise, they're worth it," Kayla said.

Lucas kept his gaze trained on Nick as he trudged toward the picnic tables, then slouched onto a bench. The boy didn't so much as glance toward the tacos, the cooler full of juice boxes or the dessert table.

"Hi!" Kayla waved her arms, dragging Lucas's attention away from Nick.

Uh oh.

Why did he feel so self-conscious all of a sudden? This was his camp. He was allowed to drop in and check on the campers.

He cleared his throat. "Hey you, looks like I'm just in time for fish tacos."

Kayla cast a pointed glance at the cluster of boys and girls gathered around the grill. "At this rate, you may have to cut in line. They're a hungry bunch."

Lucas shook his head. "What? You didn't save me one? Maybe I need to find some new friends."

Nick's dejected face flashed briefly in his mind, followed by the image of Jenna standing on the deck of the beach house, her dark hair tossed by the sea air and eyes as stormy as a tempest.

Lucas blinked. Hard.

"Good luck with that, McKinnon," Kayla said.

He peered past her toward Nick, still sitting by himself. "How's Nick doing out there?"

Kayla's eyebrows drew together. "You know him?"

"Neighbor of the month." Lucas had become accustomed to the revolving door that was the other half of the beach house. He thought he had anyway, until Jenna and her kids turned up.

"Well, he starts off strong and then just sort of gives up." Kayla fiddled with the red lanyard of the whistle around her neck. "But I'm sure he'll get there."

"I'm sure he will." Lucas nodded.

He didn't want to give Kayla the impression that he thought she wasn't doing a good job. She was great with the kids. He couldn't run the summer day camp without her.

Lucas had no reason to interfere. If Kayla thought Nick would improve on his own, chances were he would. She had far more experience with this sort of thing than Lucas did. He hadn't been lying when he'd told Nick he wasn't exactly a teacher. Yes, he owned a summer day camp, but he was strictly hands-off when it came to the campers. The camp at Tybee was a way for him to turn his love for the beach into a way to make a living. Sharing his passion for nature and the shore with the younger generation meant the world to him, but that didn't mean he wanted to get personally involved with all of the campers. Or any of them, really. He didn't need that kind of pressure.

The reasonable thing to do—the *smart* thing to do—would be to let Kayla do what she did best and just stay out of it. But as she grinned and headed toward the picnic area, Lucas found himself watching Nick again. And the sadder the little boy looked, the more the ache in Lucas's gut nagged at him.

Maybe it wasn't such a bad thing that there weren't any fish tacos left.

Lucas wasn't hungry anymore.

Just like Nick.

Jenna pushed through the screen door of the beach house and headed out onto the patio, ice-cold glass of lemonade in hand.

She paused and looked down at the picnic table, once again perfectly arranged for a productive afternoon writing session. Laptop? Check. Thesaurus? Check. Her grandpa's old typewriter for added inspiration? Check.

She sat down and started typing, eager to get at least a chapter written before it was time to pick up Nick and Ally from camp. Her deadline was beginning to weigh on her. They'd been at the beach for almost a week now, and she still hadn't made any real progress. Her manuscript was due the day before they were scheduled to drive back to Savannah. If she kept letting time slip away, she'd never make her deadline.

As much as Jenna would have liked to continue to blame Lucas, she couldn't. Since the fence had gone up, he hadn't given her any real problems. Part of her was tempted to believe she'd overreacted. But the other part of her—the sensible part that couldn't be swayed by his cute doggy-dad vibe—knew she'd been right.

Then why is your word count still so pathetic?

Jenna banged out another sentence. Her word count wasn't *that* bad. She could still finish on time. *If* she started thinking more about her plot and less about Lucas and Tank.

Which she would.

Starting right now.

She typed a third sentence and smiled to herself. *There.* She was feeling better already.

Her self-satisfaction was short-lived, though. Before she could get going on her second paragraph, a loud guitar riff interrupted the soothing beach sounds of gulls crying and waves tumbling on the shore. And this time, it wasn't coming from Lucas's side of the duplex. It seemed closer, if that was even possible.

"What the heck?" She rose from her cozy picnic bench and walked to the end of the patio to investigate.

Just beyond the dune, a beach volleyball game was in full swing. Players in swimsuits high-fived each other and batted a ball back and forth over a net anchored in the sand. Someone had propped stereo speakers nearby, making the whole scene into a perfect beach party.

And Lucas McKinnon was right there in the center of it. Because of course he was.

Jenna sighed. "Come on, man. I'm trying to work."

She waved her arms, hoping to catch his attention. Was there a universal gesture for *turn the music down?* There had to be, right?

Whether there was or wasn't didn't matter because Lucas didn't bat an eye in her direction. Nor did his friends. They were too caught up in the game to worry about Jenna and her teen fiction novel that was due in four short weeks.

She crossed her arms. She was going to have to go down there, wasn't she?

"I got it! I got it!" One of the players dove into the sand and managed to get to the ball just time.

As soon as it crossed the net, Lucas spiked it back. Jenna might have been impressed...if she hadn't had thousands of unwritten words to worry about. She stomped from the deck to the dune in record time, feet sinking into the sand as she made her way toward the noisy spectacle.

"My man!" A guy in a white tank top gave Lucas an appreciative slap on the back.

He didn't seem to notice because he was too busy staring at Jenna with a wary look on his face. "Uh oh. Here we go."

She forced a smile, since she apparently had a reputation as a complete and total killjoy. "Am I the only one who works around here?"

He laughed.

"Just kidding." They were, after all, at the beach, where people usually went for vacation. "But seriously, am I?"

She glanced toward the shore, dotted with sandcastles and beach umbrellas. Children darted in and out of the surf chasing foamy waves while a group of nearby beach-combers collected shells in a big wicker basket. Jenna let out a wistful sigh. The summer was passing by so quickly. She should be slathered in sunscreen right now with bare feet and beach hair, not chastising her neighbor for having a little fun.

"In case you haven't noticed, volleyball *is* hard work." Lucas's dimples flashed and he raked a hand through his dark hair.

"Especially when you're winning," Tank top guy chimed in.

Another player on their team shook her head. "Don't get ahead of yourself. We just started."

So Jenna was in for more of this noise all afternoon. Marvelous. "Great. Well, I just started working, and it's not going so well. So, if you could just turn the music…"

"Down a bit?" Lucas mimed turning down a volume knob.

The universal *keep it down* gesture! She knew one existed. He was totally speaking her language. For once.

"That would be awesome."

"You got it." He winked.

Her face went hot for some weird reason. She swallowed. "Yeah?"

"Yeah."

Seriously, why was she so warm all of a sudden?

He nodded, turned down the music with a few taps on his cell phone and headed back to the game.

"Great. Thanks." Well, that was a million times easier than she thought it would be.

A player on the other side of the net tossed the ball into the air, preparing to serve. "Four-four!" he yelled.

Instead of watching the ball, Lucas shot Jenna a cheeky grin. "What? Too loud?"

She mirrored his volume knob signal. "Little bit."

"We'll keep it down." The ball whizzed past his head.

Jenna couldn't help but laugh. As she made her way back over the dune, she could have sworn she felt Lucas's gaze on her back, as warm as the summer sun.

But she refused to look. She was probably imagining things, anyway. Just because they were finally getting along didn't mean he thought of her as anyone but the cranky lady who'd moved in next door.

Correction: the cranky *mom* who'd moved in next door.

Lucas was only being polite. He tolerated her kids about as well as she tolerated his slacker surfer lifestyle. And nothing was more important in the world to Jenna than Nick and Ally.

Whatever he thought about her, he kindly kept the noise to a minimum for the rest of the afternoon. Once Jenna could hear herself think, she managed to make some actual progress on her manuscript. After a few intense timed writing sprints, she had a shiny new chapter under her belt. She just wished she could come up with a solid ending to the story. That major detail was still eluding her.

When at last she'd written ten pages—ten!—she couldn't wait to pick up the kids. She considered a few potential endings as she steered the car along the sand-swept road to the beach camp. The trip was a slow crawl through summer, island traffic, but she arrived just as Nick, Ally and the other campers were making their way from the shore to the camp's wooden deck with beach towels wrapped around their slim shoulders and popsicles in their hands. On the way home, Ally gushed about the new turtle nest they'd discovered high up on the dunes and the tracks the mama turtle had left in the sand—deep trenches winding from the shore to the nest and back out to sea again.

While the kids showered and changed into fresh clothes, Jenna set three place settings on the picnic table out on the deck. Then she fired up the grill for steaks, Nick's favorite. By the time the kids were ready, she'd managed to add fresh-squeezed lemonade, salad, veggies and cold sliced watermelon. The perfect summer spread.

"Here's to my beach warriors and a fantastic summer at camp." Jenna raised her glass.

"How long is it again?" Nick stared down at his plate.

Jenna frowned. He'd been awfully quiet since he'd trudged to the car after camp with his damp towel slung around his neck. She'd thought he was simply tired after a busy day in the pool and at the beach, content to let Ally dominate the conversation. Now she wasn't so sure.

"Can we cheers now?" Ally's glass of lemonade hovered above the table.

Jenna tapped hers against it. "Yes. Cheers!"

Nick clinked his glass too, but instead of taking a sip, he sat staring over Jenna's shoulder toward the shore. "Maybe I should just learn to surf instead."

This was new. He'd talked about nothing but swim team for the past year and a half. His heart had been set on making the qualifying time at the trial at the end of summer, so he'd be prepared going into tryouts for the school swim team in the fall.

Worry gnawed at Jenna as she dished salad onto his plate. "Why would you want to do that? We don't normally live near the beach."

Nick shrugged. "I don't know. Our neighbor does it."

So this was about Lucas. Of course. Why hadn't she seen it coming?

She glanced over her shoulder to follow Nick's gaze. Sure enough, Lucas was making his way over the dune with a surfboard tucked under his arm. He was wearing his wetsuit and flip-flops. Again.

No wonder Nick had started looking at him as if he was some kind of hero. His life was one big beach volleyball game. As nice as it seemed, it wasn't exactly realistic. Or responsible.

Or safe.

It had been a while since Nick had a male role model to look up to, though. Under the terms of the divorce, Jenna had primary custody of the kids, but she encouraged them to see their dad as much as possible. She wanted them to have a normal, happy childhood, despite the fact that their parents were no longer together. But her ex-husband traveled all over the world for work. Last month, he'd been in Sweden, and now he'd be in Tokyo for the rest of the summer. Jenna knew Nick missed him. Having a man in such close proximity probably wasn't the worst thing in the world.

Still, the last thing she needed was Nick on a surfboard. She worried enough about him swimming across the pool without tethering him to a heavy board and putting him in the ocean. Maybe she should see if Ian could teach him how to build something instead.

"I'd rather you *not* try anything our

neighbor does." Jenna arched an eyebrow. "Ever."

"Okay." Nick grinned. "Now tell me how you really feel."

Jenna shook her head. "No. That isn't a feeling thing, it's a health and safety thing."

She didn't have any *feelings* about Lucas one way or another.

"Suuuure." Nick's grin widened and he bit into a slice of watermelon.

"What? It is." Of course it was. She was only being logical...a rational, reasonable adult. Because someone in the beach house needed to act like a grown-up.

Still, a change of subject was in order. For some reason, she wasn't sure she wanted her kids prying into her thoughts where Lucas was concerned. She wasn't altogether sure she wanted to pry into them herself.

"Who wants steak?" She smiled brightly and passed the platter across the table to Nick.

Luckily, a sirloin fresh off the grill was enough to make him forget about becoming Lucas's mini-me.

At least temporarily.

Tank could've smelled Jenna's steaks from a mile away. Unfortunately for Lucas, her sirloins were much closer in proximity and, therefore, all the more tempting.

At first, Tank's interest in what was happening on the opposite side of the picket fence was limited to a few subtle twitches of his nose. As Lucas sprawled on one of his patio chairs with a book in his hand and his feet propped on the driftwood coffee cable, Tank tiptoed closer and closer to the fence. Lucas, pretending not to notice, hoped his pup would give up on the idea of a doggy bag. The odds of that happening were slim to none, considering Tank was supposed to be the entire reason the fence had been constructed in the first place.

Right. Lucas still wasn't buying that flimsy explanation. He saw the way Jenna Turner looked at him when she thought he wasn't paying attention—like she'd forgotten all about his messy porch and lack of houseplants. Every now and then she actually smiled, as if maybe he wasn't the absolute last person she'd wish to stumble upon in her shared outdoor shower. In those moments, he had a sneaking suspicion that the fence had more to do with him than it did Tank. In all likelihood, the poor dog was just an innocent bystander.

An innocent bystander with a sudden craving for steak.

Tank glanced at the smoke billowing in the air from the other side of the fence, then stared pointedly at Lucas. When Lucas failed to produce a filet mignon out of thin air, Tank let out a pitiful whine.

"Okay, I can take a hint, bud." Lucas put down his book, headed toward the house and held the door open so Tank could follow him inside.

The dog's tail was a little white blur of glee as Lucas got his bowl down from the cupboard and filled it with food. Tank's excitement took a serious hit when he saw nothing but plain kibble in his bowl, and he shot another soulful look at Lucas.

"Believe me, I'd rather be eating steak too." Lucas tossed a biscuit into his bowl. It was a poor substitution, but Tank happily scarfed it down. "How about we head out to the beach with a shovel instead?"

Tank's tail started wagging again, which Lucas took as a yes. Once the dog bowl was empty and Lucas had made himself a sand-wich—also a poor substitution for sirloin—he threw on a hoodie and grabbed the tall shovel he took down to the shore most evenings. Tank scampered at his heels, and they made their way down the outdoor steps of the beach house. Lucas couldn't help venturing a glance over the top of the fence, but Jenna and her kids had apparently finished eating dinner. An animated fish was swimming across the television in the living room while

Nick and Ally sat on the sofa with a big bowl of popcorn between them.

Lucas wondered briefly what their mother was up to. For some reason, he kept forgetting that they'd gotten off on the wrong foot—maybe because he admired the close relationship she had with her kids.

Lucas would have given anything to have that sort of closeness with his father when he'd been growing up. Jenna was obviously very serious about her writing career. Her frequent noise complaints had gotten that message across loud and clear, but she was even more serious about her parenting. Yes, she was a tad on the controlling side. There was no denying that, but he'd also witnessed the easy affection between her, Ally and Nick, and at times it made him feel oddly hollow inside. Wistful.

But then he'd catch another glimpse of the fence and remember he and Jenna were not interested in each other. Besides, Tank was all he needed.

The dog yipped and ran circles around Lucas's feet when they reached the foot of the stairs. Their evening beach ritual was one of the dog's favorite things.

"Lookie here, bud. We already found one," Lucas said as he stepped off the wooden deck onto the cool sand of the dune.

Tank barked into the empty hole in

the ground, his yips echoing in the purple
shadows of twilight. Lucas scooped a generous portion of sand back into the hole and
tapped it down with the head of his shovel
while Tank darted back and forth through
the sea oats in search of another hole.

"Don't dogs usually dig holes?" Jenna's
voice seemed softer with the eventide, but it
was most definitely her. Lucas turned around
and saw her lingering at the foot of the stairs
with a trash bag in her hands. Of course
she was doing chores. She looked past him
toward Tank. "I swear it looks like he wants
to help you fill them in."

Lucas squinted at his dog, dancing mer-
rily around a wide crater in the damp sand
closer to the shore. "He does, actually."

"Wait." Jenna tossed the plastic bag into
the big, shared trash can on the corner of the
deck, kicked off her flip-flops and joined him
on the dune. "Seriously?"

Lucas shrugged. "It's kind of our thing."

He gave the hole he'd just filled in another pat with his shovel, fully expecting her to
turn around and head back upstairs. When
she stayed put instead, he felt himself smile.

"It's for the turtles," he said by way of
explanation.

She tilted her head, and her hair fell over
her shoulder in a dark curtain of beachy
waves.

For one nonsensical second, Lucas wondered what it would be like to reach out and wind a loose curl around his fingertips. A completely irrational notion that he blamed on the full moon shining bright over the ocean's salty waves.

"The turtles?" She gave him a slow smile that built with each passing second.

It happened to be Lucas's favorite kind of smile. He nodded. "You've probably heard the island is a nesting ground for endangered sea turtles. We're still early in the season, but the eggs will start to hatch soon and when they do, the turtle hatchlings have to crawl from the dune to the ocean. It can be a treacherous journey for a turtle no bigger than a silver dollar."

Jenna blinked. "So you and Tank go around filling in holes in the sand every night, so the baby turtles can make it safely to the ocean?"

Was that really so hard to believe? The island was his home. He loved it with his whole heart. "We might miss a night here and there."

She shook her head. "I just..."

"What?" He speared the shovel into the sand and leaned against it, studying her. She was gaping at him as if he'd just surfed straight into her living room on a loggerhead turtle's back.

81

"Just wow." Jenna took a deep breath. "That's so...sweet."

"I'm not all bad," he said.

He had no clue why he was trying to convince her that he was a decent guy despite his lack of houseplants.

"I didn't say you were."

Their gazes locked, and for a long moment neither of them said a word. Lucas was so focused on the charged silence that he didn't notice Tank bounding toward them until the dog planted himself at Jenna's feet. Before Lucas could stop what was about to happen, Tank gave his coat a hard shake, spraying Jenna with sand.

She jumped backward, squealing and wiping bits of sand from her white shorts.

So much for their almost-truce.

"Sorry about that," Lucas said, but his apology was drowned out by Nick and Ally calling down from the balcony above them.

"Mom," they said in unison.

"Are you okay?" Ally asked. She sounded like she might be talking around a mouthful of chocolate.

Jenna glared at Lucas, even though, technically, Tank had been the troublemaker.

This time.

"I'm fine," she said sharply. Then she squared her shoulders, spun on her heel and marched back toward enemy territory.

After a full week of summer camp, the kids were exhausted. They both slept in the following morning, allowing Jenna to get a few pages written before breakfast. The house seemed too quiet without Ally's usual morning chatter, so at around eight o'clock Jenna finally tiptoed between their bunk beds and pulled open the curtains.

"Rise and shine, monkeys! It's the weekend." Sunlight streamed into the brightly decorated bedroom.

It was an awfully cute space, but Jenna was no longer such a fan of the surfboard-themed bunks. She was having very confusing feelings about surfers.

Nick sat up, rubbing his eyes. "What time is it?"

Ally groaned. "I'm hungry."

"Then I guess we'd better hurry up and figure out what we want to do today. We could go to the sand dunes or the butterfly park?" Jenna glanced back and forth between Nick and Ally. Neither appeared thrilled at her suggestions.

Nick yawned. "Can't we just go to the beach?"

A day at the beach made the most sense, seeing as it was practically right outside their door. But Jenna was really hoping to steer

Nick's thoughts away from his surfing fantasy before it took root.

"Yeah, I guess we could go to the beach," she said. But she still wasn't giving up on the butterfly park. Butterflies, after all, were completely innocuous. "What do you want to do, Ally?"

Her little girl grinned. "I want to go to the beach."

Jenna knew when she was outnumbered. "All right, the beach it is. Let's do it."

An hour later, she was halfway buried in sand—not a butterfly in sight. It wasn't so bad, really. The ocean shimmered in the morning light, sunshine glinting off the water like scattered gemstones. She closed her eyes and tilted her face toward the warm sun, letting the sound of rushing waves ease the tension in her neck and shoulders. The air smelled like salt and sea—the sweet perfume of her childhood summers.

Jenna couldn't believe she'd been at the beach for a week already and this was the first time she'd had a chance to wiggle her toes in the sand. If Ally had her way, she wouldn't be able to wiggle them much longer, though. She'd already completely buried Jenna from her waist to her ankles, and she'd vowed not to stop until she'd transformed her mother into a sandy mermaid.

"Wow, you're doing a really thorough job," Jenna said.

Ally patted the sand around her torso more firmly in place as she surveyed her handiwork. Her brow furrowed. "I can still see your toes."

"Maybe we should let them breathe a little bit."

"Nope. I need another bucket." Ally plunged her plastic shovel into the sand.

Jenna laughed, but then she spotted Lucas farther down the beach and grew pensive. "Is that our neighbor out there?"

Of course it was. He had all the standard Lucas accessories—surfboard, wetsuit and lazy grin, complete with charming dimples. Watching him stand at the water's edge with foam swirling around his ankles made her heart beat hard for some strange reason.

Ally squinted at him in the distance and then dumped a fresh load of sand onto Jenna's feet. "He's not a criminal, Mom. Why don't you like him?"

"What?" Jenna blinked and tore her gaze away from Lucas. "I didn't say I didn't like him."

Ally scooped more sand into her bucket. "He has to be nice. His dog is nice."

Ah, if only such logic could be trusted. "I think owners look like their dogs, sweetie. I'm not sure they act like them."

Maybe that was a good thing. She wasn't

sure she wanted her human neighbor pawing through her manuscript.

On second thought, she definitely didn't want that.

But she also didn't want Ally to think she disliked Lucas because she didn't. She just disliked his self-purported bachelor lifestyle. Every time she started to cave and think he might be a great guy, she remembered what he'd said about keeping her kids contained.

I'll keep my furry kid on this side if you keep your kids on that side.

What kind of person had a soft spot for baby turtles but didn't like kids?

Then again, who built a fence to keep a cute dog off their side of the patio?

There was more to it than that.

She needed a barrier around her heart even more than she needed one around her living space. Had the divorce really been four long years ago? Sometimes she felt as tender and wounded as if it had happened yesterday. She felt like she was walking around with her broken heart on display for the entire world to see, and she just needed to hide for a while. To rest. Trying to keep everything in her life in perfect working order was exhausting, and somehow when Lucas was around, Jenna felt more unsettled than ever.

She didn't have a thing to feel guilty about but her throat grew thick all the same.

She swallowed hard and concentrated all

her attention on the shells Ally was pressing
into the sand around her legs.

"Where's my mermaid tail?"

Lucas shielded his face from the sun with
his hand and watched the waves pound the
sand. He couldn't have asked for better surfing conditions. The water was glassy with a
fine spray coming off the tops of the waves,
breaking in a nice, steady line parallel to the
shore.

All signs pointed toward a great morning,
but he should probably act fast. The surf report predicted a stormy afternoon.

He waded farther into the water, just
past the swirl of foam where the sandpipers
darted in and out of the surf.

And then he paused.

A little boy was coming out of the water,
carrying a boogie board. The board had the
same shark pattern as the swim trunks Nick
wore yesterday at camp. And the boy had the
same slender frame that reminded Lucas so
much of himself at that age.

Lucas's heart gave a little squeeze and
before he fully realized what he was doing, he
grabbed hold of his board and met the boy at
the water's edge. "Hey buddy, how's it going?
How are your lap times coming?"

Nick's answer was flat. Lifeless. "They're fine."

"Fine? What's that supposed to mean?" Lucas said.

Nick shrugged. "Doesn't matter. I'm not trying out for swim team anymore."

Lucas wasn't buying it. Nick wouldn't have asked him for help if making the team wasn't important to him. "Because you don't want to, or because you're afraid to try?"

Lucas knew a little something about the latter.

You don't want to get involved, remember?

He didn't...he *wouldn't*...but maybe he could just give the kid a pep talk. What harm would that do?

"Listen," Nick said, suddenly sounding like a tiny adult. "I know this isn't your 'thing.'"

Ouch. "Did I say that?"

Nick nodded. "Twice."

Guilty as charged. But maybe it wasn't too late to provide some encouragement.

Lucas shifted his weight from one foot to the other. "You know, a very wise dude once said 'you miss one hundred percent of the shots you don't take.'"

Nick gave him a blank look. "Is that some sort of Yoda quote?"

"No. That's a pretty good guess, but no."

So much for his genius pep talk. "It was Wayne Gretzky."

Surely the kid knew who The Great One was.

"Does he surf?" Nick asked.

Lucas sighed.

"That's not the point. The point is, if you're interested..." He took a deep breath. Was he really going to do this? "...if my schedule lightens up..."

"My mom said you don't have a schedule," Nick countered.

Oh, she did, did she? "Your mom doesn't know everything."

Nick let out a laugh.

"Like I said, I've been thinking. If you're interested, I could give you some pointers."

The little boy's face lit up like it was Christmas morning. "Really?"

"Yeah." What had he just gotten himself into? "I mean, don't get too excited. Just like twenty minutes here and there. Nothing major."

"Cool!" Nick bit back a smile and did his best to imitate Lucas's casual demeanor. "I mean, yeah. Sure. I'd be up for that."

If Lucas didn't know better, he would have thought the boy looked up to him. It wasn't possible though, was it? He hadn't given Nick any actual help.

Yet.

"All right, we'll figure it out." Lucas held up his hand.

Nick slapped it in a high five.

Lucas didn't know what to add at that point. He'd already said more than he'd planned to, and honestly he wasn't even sure he was up to the task of helping Nick. He'd be better off sticking to things he actually knew a little bit about, like surfing.

Plus, he had a feeling Jenna might not approve of his offer to give the kid a few pointers. He probably should have cleared it with her first, but it was too late now.

As he slid past Nick to head back to the water, the boy called after him. "Hey, Lucas?"

He stopped. *What now?* Lucas no longer trusted himself to think straight around the poor kid. Next thing he knew, he'd probably be volunteering to coach his swim team in the fall.

That wasn't quite what Nick had in mind, though. "Can we maybe not tell my mom about this? I'm not sure she'd like it."

Lucas followed Nick's gaze as he shot a meaningful glance toward the spot on the beach where Jenna was half-buried in the sand. Lucas was so accustomed to seeing her pounding away on her laptop at the picnic table that he hadn't noticed her.

She and Ally were just a stone's throw away, surrounded by a colorful collection of plastic shovels and buckets. Jenna wore a bright green swimsuit and an elaborately crafted mermaid tail carved out of sand and covered in delicate shells. When she tossed her head back and laughed at something her daughter said, Lucas's breath caught in his throat. Summer looked good on Jenna Turner.

Then she glanced his direction and the tender curve of her lips flattened into a straight, unimpressed line. Lucas looked away.

The kid had a point. After all, Jenna had disliked him so much at first that she'd put up a barrier between them...even if, sometimes, he got the feeling that her opinion of him was changing.

"Mum's the word," he said. "You get it?"

Nick rolled his eyes at the terrible pun.

"Sorry, I had to." Lucas shrugged and it wasn't until he walked away that he realized what he'd just done.

He'd made an actual dad joke.

Chapter Five

*A*FTER THINKING ON IT ALL night, Lucas was convinced that the best way to help Nick with his swim times was to coach him while he was at day camp. Otherwise, Jenna was sure to find out.

He'd also determined that keeping her out of the loop was probably a mistake. A *big* one. But he'd already promised Nick he wouldn't say anything to her about it, and he didn't want to go back on his word.

Lucas could help Nick. He knew he could. He also knew what it felt like to be smaller than the rest of the kids his age, to be slower. Always a step behind.

So even though he knew it was probably a terrible idea, he showed up at camp bright and early the next morning with a stopwatch around his neck and a plan to get Nick going a little faster.

"All right, now to strengthen your stroke you need to learn to swim like a surfer." Lucas glanced down at the middle lane of the swimming pool and back up at Nick.

The boy's slim arms dangled at his sides. "Seriously?"

Okay, maybe that wasn't the most useful advice for someone who didn't know how to surf. "Just focus on shortening the number of strokes it takes for you to get to the end of the pool, and I promise it'll help you catch lots of waves."

Nick shrugged one shoulder. "But I don't surf."

Maybe he should stop with the surfing analogies. "That's not the point. Do you want to break 1:18 or not?"

Nick let out a defeated sigh.

Trust me, kid. "Go!"

Lucas watched as Nick dove off the starting block and began kicking his legs furiously as he made his way across the pool. He reached the halfway point in just four or five strokes.

Lucas checked the digital display on his stopwatch and smiled to himself. They were making progress already.

He looked up when he felt someone give his arm a playful jab.

Kayla smiled at him. "Wow. Are you getting soft in your old age? This helping-kids thing is new for you."

"He's just one kid." Lucas held up a pointer finger. "Just one time."

He told her about Jenna and the fence at the beach house because he didn't need her getting any crazy ideas. Lucas wasn't the official camp swim coach all of a sudden, nor was he getting soft. And he definitely wasn't going to be spouting off any more dad jokes. Nick's mom barely tolerated his existence. Helping the kid was truly no big deal.

"That's what you think, easy-breezy, right?" She arched an eyebrow.

Exactly, Lucas thought. *Easy-breezy*. He'd help the kid get his time fast enough to make the swim team, and then he'd go back to worrying about no one but himself. Nick would be long gone in a month, anyway.

So would Jenna.

Kayla shook her head. "Let me tell ya, once they go in for the hug it's all over. Next thing you know, you're wearing mouse ears at Disneyland because you couldn't bear to say no."

He let out a laugh. She couldn't be more off base. He was coaching Nick, not hugging him. There'd be no Disneyland, and *definitely* no mouse ears.

"Are you done?" he asked.

"Maybe." She shrugged, but the sparkle of amusement in her eyes told him she wasn't finished teasing him about his sudden interest in his temporary neighbors. Not by a long shot.

Someone needed to remember who was the boss around here. He ruffled her hair like he would an annoying little sister.

"Stop it!" She retaliated with a punch to his stomach. "Stop!"

He held up his hands in surrender and she darted around him to catch up with the campers who were headed toward the picnic area for snack time.

He'd figured Kayla would have something to say when she found out he was helping Nick. Considering how reluctant Lucas had always been to get involved with the campers, he'd gotten off pretty easy. But he had a feeling he hadn't heard the last of it.

Super.

He couldn't worry about Kayla or her ridiculous mouse ear references now. He needed to check Nick's freestyle stroke before Jenna showed up, but when he turned back toward the water, there she was.

She was standing on the other side of the pool with her sunglasses in her hand, frozen in place with the strangest look on her face. The second he met her gaze, she looked away.

Relief coursed through Lucas. If she'd realized he was there for Nick, she might be angry about it. Besides, she'd gone too wide-eyed to be mad. If Lucas hadn't known better, he would have thought she was...jealous.

No. He frowned. *Impossible.*

Jenna's gaze flicked toward Kayla and then back at him. The flush in her cheeks deepened a shade and she shoved her sunglasses back in place.

Maybe not so impossible, after all.

Living at the beach full-time for the past five years had taught Lucas a thing or two about island life. Contrary to whatever Jenna Turner liked to believe, not all of those things involved lying around in a hammock or annoying his neighbors. Case in point: he'd become an expert at constructing beach bonfires.

He was kind of famous for it, actually. All the year-round Tybee residents looked forward to his casual campfire nights, which he held once a month or so during the summer. He'd build a big fire, then toss a few blankets, beach chairs and extra logs around, and whoever showed up was welcome. Lucas usually strummed his guitar for a bit. Sometimes, old Sam from the fish joint down at the pier would tell stories about ghost ships and the pirates who roamed the high seas of the Georgia coast. According to Tybee lore, Blackbeard's treasure was buried somewhere on the island.

Lucas had his doubts. Tank had done enough digging at the beach that he probably would have come across it at one point or another. Of course now that Lucas actually *needed* a three-foot wide hole on the shore, Tank was too busy gnawing on a driftwood stick to contribute.

"You can pitch in any time now," Lucas said as he heaved another shovelful of fine white sand over his shoulder.

Tank's tail wagged at the sound of Lucas's voice, but he didn't bother looking up from the wedge of driftwood.

"It's okay, bud. I forgive you." After all, Tank was his best friend. And besides, Lucas wasn't the type of man to come between a dog and his stick.

He speared his shovel into the sand again. The secret to a great beach bonfire was digging the perfect pit. It had to be far enough away from the water line to survive high tide, and it had to be deep enough to protect the flames from the wind. Lucas also liked to dig down far enough so that the bottom of his pit was always lined with damp, heavy sand, which prevented the fire from spreading. Safety first.

He was still moving dry sand as fine as powder, so he knew he still had a ways to go, when all of a sudden Jenna's kids appeared. They hovered near the outer ring of the pit, peering into it. Each of them held a colorful beach pail—Ally's was a bright, sunny yellow and Nick's was blue.

Lucas had a feeling he knew what was coming next.

"Wow, that's a big hole." Ally's eyes went wide. She plucked a plastic shovel out of the bucket in her hand. "Do you want some help?"

Bingo.

"Sure. The more, the merrier." Granted, the tiny shovels they had looked about as effective as digging with teaspoons, but every little bit helped.

Ally dropped to her knees and got to work, peppering Tank with a constant stream of chatter as she hauled sand out of the hole, two or three grains at a time. The dog's attention stayed focused on his stick, but his tail swept back and forth, moving more sand around than either of the kids' plastic tools managed to accomplish.

Nick sighed and cast a longing glance at Lucas's aluminum scoop shovel. "Can I borrow yours?"

"No, you may not," someone said.

The voice came from somewhere behind Lucas, and he was so certain who it belonged to that he would have wagered Tank's stick on it.

"Mom." Nick swallowed. "Hi."

Lucas turned around to find her standing in her pretty emerald-hued swimsuit—the one that reminded him so much of a mermaid, even without the sandy tail—with her arms full of more beach toys.

"I'm so sorry. They told me they wanted to come out here and build a sandcastle. Clearly that was just a ruse to help you with..." Her brow furrowed as she inspected the fire pit. "...whatever this is."

"It's a fire pit," he said.

"A fire pit?" she echoed.

"Cool!" Nick beamed while Ally ignored all of them and kept talking to Tank. She'd abandoned her shovel in favor of picking the sand out of his fur while he gnawed away at his driftwood.

"Yes." Lucas shrugged. "I'm having a bonfire tonight."

He could've left it at that. But somewhere in the back of his head he was still thinking about the look on her face when she'd seen him messing around with Kayla at the pool earlier.

Who was he kidding? It wasn't in the back of his head at all. It had been right at the forefront of his mind, the starring attraction of his thoughts the entire time he'd been digging the hole.

"You should come," he heard himself say.

She blinked. "I, um..."

Her gaze flitted to Nick, then Ally.

"All of you," Lucas clarified.

"Yessss." Nick let loose with a fist pump.

"I don't know." Jenna gnawed at her bottom lip. "We wouldn't want to impose."

"It's no imposition. It's just a bonfire." It was a spur of the moment invitation, so it shouldn't matter whether or not she said yes. But Lucas hoped she did. He hoped more than he wanted to admit.

At long last, Tank looked up from his stick. His scruffy head swiveled back and forth from Lucas to Jenna as if he was as invested in her answer as Lucas had somehow become.

She was going to say no. He could feel it.

"Mom, please," Nick begged.

"Yeah, Mom. It'll be fun." Ally pointed at the pit. "We already helped dig the hole."

That was debatable.

Lucas scrubbed his hand over his mouth to disguise his smirk and also to prevent himself from issuing another ill-conceived invitation. Like maybe even a date.

"Maybe." Jenna attempted a nonchalant shrug. Her constant state of anxiety was beginning to fascinate him for some strange reason. He wondered what it would take to make her throw her head back and laugh out loud.

He couldn't picture it, but he knew without a doubt it would be a breathtaking sight.

Nick and Ally sighed audibly. "*Maybe?*"

"Good. I'll see you later, then." Lucas turned his attention back to digging. He knew better than to press his luck. "Maybe."

Jenna's *maybe* had been mom code for *no, absolutely not*. Unfortunately, Ally and Nick hadn't caught on.

They were relentless. The bonfire was all they talked about over dinner, and the more they pressed, the more Jenna began to realize that she didn't have a legitimate reason for turning down Lucas's invitation.

Not a reason she felt comfortable sharing with Nick and Ally, anyway.

She was still reeling from the strange pang she'd felt earlier at the pool as she'd watched Lucas laughing and joking around with the camp counselor. The sight had caught her completely off guard—so off guard that she hadn't bothered to wonder why Lucas was at the pool in the first place. She'd been far too busy trying to figure out why the idea that he and Kayla might be a couple bothered her.

Because it did. It bothered her a lot. If she didn't know better, she might even believe she was jealous.

Nope. She rummaged through one of the kitchen cabinets while Ally and Nick cleared the table. *Definitely not jealous.*

The very idea was absurd. Why should she care if Lucas and Kayla were a couple?

Were they a couple?

It didn't matter. She wasn't interested in Lucas, and just to prove it to herself, she was going to relent and take Ally and Nick to his bonfire.

Aha! She finally located the bag of jumbo marshmallows she'd brought to the beach in anticipation of s'mores. It was tucked behind the pancake mix and Ally's big container of chocolate chips.

Jenna plucked the bag from the cabinet and held it up in the air. "Okay, who's ready for a bonfire?"

"You mean we're really going?" In his excitement, Nick nearly dropped the stack of plates he was carrying to the sink.

"Sure," Jenna said, trying her best to sound nonchalant. "Why not?"

Ally and Nick exchanged a meaningful glance.

Great. They definitely thought she didn't like him, even after she'd done her best to convince Ally otherwise when she'd made her "criminal" comment on the beach the other day. Going to the bonfire was definitely the right call.

"Why don't you two grab your sweat-shirts while I finish cleaning up and then we'll head down?" Jenna rinsed the plates and stacked them in the dishwasher while the kids raced upstairs to get ready.

A cool breeze had blown in with the tide and the moon glittered high in the sky, reigning over the shore, making the night seem as dark and smooth as velvet. The kids were snug in their sweatshirts. Jenna threw on a cardigan, but a shiver still coursed through her as they made their way over the dune. The beach seemed like such a different place at night. Quiet. Intimate.

Lucas's bonfire was a shimmer of orange on the horizon, and as they drew closer, Jenna heard the soft strum of music. It wasn't until she and the kids had reached the circle of beach chairs around the fire pit that she realized Lucas was the source of the soothing melody.

He smiled at her from across the flames as he strummed an acoustic guitar. Tank sat at Lucas's feet with his head cocked at a jaunty angle, one ear up and one ear down. They couldn't have looked more darling together if they'd tried.

Jenna glanced around. A teenager with red hair parted into two braids sat immediately to his left, and on Lucas's other side, a guy wearing a tank top sipped a bottle of beer. There were easily two dozen people around the fire, some on blankets, others standing and swaying to the music.

Standing there in her jeans and her mom-cardigan, Jenna suddenly felt a hundred years old. What was she doing there?

Proving you don't care who Lucas McKinnon dates, remember?

"I don't think we have enough marshmallows for everyone," Ally said, glancing down at the plastic bag in her hands.

"I actually don't think there's enough room for us, sweetie," Jenna said, wanting nothing more than to bolt back to the beach house.

"Sure there is," Nick countered, waving at Lucas.

Lucas waved back. "Hey, you guys want to squeeze in?"

Ally and Nick answered simultaneously. "Yeah!"

Before she could stop them, they sprinted toward the group of people around the fire.

Jenna stayed rooted in place. Her cheeks grew warm, which she blamed on the heat of the fire. It definitely wasn't because Lucas was looking at her.

She swallowed. "It looks like you're having a party. We can just come back."

"Trust me, you'd know if we were having a party." Lucas nodded at the guy beside him, motioning for him to make room on the log that served as a bench. "Scoot over."

He moved to one of the blankets on the sand, and the young woman with the red braids did the same. Nick and Ally plopped down on either side of Lucas as if they belonged there...as if Lucas *wanted* them close by. Warmth filled Jenna's chest.

"Who wants marshmallows?" Ally raised the bag in the air, and all around the bonfire hands went up.

"See." Lucas caught Jenna's gaze and cast a meaningful glance at the log beside Ally. "Plenty of room."

Jenna took a deep breath. "Yeah."

It no longer mattered whether she felt out of place or not. She couldn't very well flee and leave her kids behind.

She sat down. While the fire warmed her face, Lucas put down his guitar and helped Ally spear marshmallows onto long metal skewers. Nick jumped up, volunteering to pass them around. By the time Jenna bit into a soft, warm marshmallow, she'd actually begun to enjoy herself.

A cozy hush fell over the group, and soon the only sounds that could be heard were the crackling fire and the lullaby of waves crashing onto the shore.

This is nice. Jenna couldn't remember

the last time she'd experienced a campfire. Maybe when she'd been Ally's age? Had it really been that long?

Even Tank seemed charmed by the tranquil atmosphere. He gave up on begging for marshmallows to stretch out on a red buffalo-checked blanket near the warm glow of the flames. Within seconds, his little doggy chest rose and fell with the gentle rhythm of sleep.

Ally peered at him as she roasted a marshmallow over the fire. "Can I wake him up?"

Lucas aimed a meaningful glance at Tank. "Do you see how his eyelids are fluttering? That means he's about reached his REM cycle."

Ally's face went blank. "His what?"

Jenna figured she should probably save Lucas from having to explain the stages of the sleep cycle. "Ally, honey. Why don't we leave Mr. Tank alone?"

"But Daddy said I could get a dog," she protested.

"I'm sure he did, honey. But a dog share might be a little tough right now. We've talked about this." Jenna loved being a mom, but it wasn't the easiest thing in the world, especially since the divorce.

She'd never seen it coming. She'd always assumed that her marriage was solid...

happy. Granted, her dreams of being a novelist had sort of taken a backseat during the relationship. When she'd finally decided to pursue writing fiction, Robert hadn't hesitated to tell her she was wasting her time. But she'd assumed those instances had just been growing pains. Besides, she loved being an author just as much as she loved being a mom.

A wife.

In retrospect she realized she and Robert were better off as friends, but at the time, she'd been stunned to learn he wanted out. And now, deep down, she knew that part of the reason she liked to keep her household so organized was because it made her feel like she was in complete control, like she'd never be blindsided by anything ever again.

Life wasn't so simple, though. Still, she wasn't sure she was up to the challenge of adding a dog to the mix.

Ally sighed. "Can't you just change your mind?"

"She doesn't do that," Nick said.

Jenna was appalled. Did her kids really think she was that inflexible?

She liked to keep her word. Isn't that what she was supposed to do as a parent? She wanted to create a stable and safe home for her kids, but Nick and Ally were making her sound rigid and overly strict in front of half the population of Tybee. In front of *Lucas*.

His face was a complete blank as he stared into the fire, no doubt ruminating again on how much she needed to relax.

She wished a wave would crash onto the shore and sweep her away.

"How about this?" Lucas turned toward Ally. Jenna dreaded whatever was about to come out of his mouth. "How about you take Tank for a walk tomorrow morning. Would you like that?"

Jenna nearly fell off her log. Had he just offered to do something nice for one of her kids?

"Awesome!" Ally's face split into a wide grin.

"Wow. That *is* pretty nice." Jenna stared at Lucas. Was it her imagination, or did the firelight make his eyes dance?

He arched a brow. "You sound surprised."

"I'm not surprised. I'm just..." She struggled for something to say because the word on the tip of her tongue was *charmed*. It was such an unexpectedly sweet offer, and Lucas was anything but sweet. Maybe the marshmallows were going to her head.

While she sat there, speechless, his gaze flicked over her shoulder. Jenna turned to see what had caught his attention and sure enough, three gorgeous, slender women were approaching the campfire. Was that Kayla, the camp counselor in the middle?

Of course it was, and she wasn't wearing anything resembling a mom-cardigan.

Now this *isn't a bit surprising.* Mr. Bachelor strikes again.

"Actually, I think we should get going," Jenna said.

Lucas didn't seem to hear.

"We should?" Nick inspected the marshmallow on the end of his skewer, still only half-melted.

"Yeah." Jenna nodded. *Help me out here, kid.*

"Right. We should. 'Cause I'm pretty wiped, and I've been working on a new swim technique. It's pretty cool actually." Nick grinned at Lucas.

Jenna didn't know what he was talking about, and right that second, she didn't care. She just wanted to get back to the beach house before she had to watch Lucas and Kayla engage in another adorable, carefree frolic.

"Oh, yeah?" Lucas said.

"Yeah." Nick nodded. "And my mom likes to watch *Real Housewives* before..."

"Okay, we're going." Jenna flew to her feet. "Let's go, please. *Now.*"

Nick thought she was suddenly eager to

get home so she could watch bad reality television? Great. Now she sounded even more pathetic than she felt.

"What? You do." Nick shrugged as she did her best to usher the kids back toward the beach house.

"Good night," Lucas said, and the smile in his voice made her mortification all the more complete.

"Good night," she muttered without meeting his gaze.

Ally saved her goodbyes for the dog. "Good night, Tank. See you in the morning."

Tank's eye opened and he peered after her. She practically floated as she headed toward the dune.

Jenna, on the other hand, felt like she was slinking away in humiliation.

Real Housewives? Really, Nick?

She pulled her sweater tighter around her frame, snuggling into it she snuck one last look at the scene around the bonfire. Big mistake.

"I'm glad you could make it," Lucas said as Kayla sat beside him, right where Ally had been just moments before. He glanced up at one of Kayla's pretty friends and patted the space recently vacated by Nick. "There's room on this side."

Jenna hastened her steps.

Real Housewives suddenly didn't sound

so bad. It was definitely preferable to the real-life version of *The Bachelor* starring Lucas McKinnon.

Chapter Six

LUCAS WAS VAGUELY AWARE OF a knocking sound on his front door the next morning, but he kept his eyes closed and burrowed deeper into his sofa.

The noise couldn't be a visitor. Who got up this early at the beach? No one, that's who. It had to be a something else—a confused pelican, maybe?

Knock, knock, knock.

There it was again, and to Lucas's dismay, it indeed sounded like it was coming from regular human knuckles.

He cracked one eye open and looked at Tank stretched out beside him. "You want to get that, buddy?"

Tank didn't budge.

Knock, knock, knock. Whoever was pounding on the door wasn't giving up.

"All right, all right. I'm coming. I'm coming." Lucas dragged himself off the couch and gave Tank a parting scratch behind his ears. "Some guard dog you are."

He glanced out the window on the way to the door. Ally stood on his porch, waving at him with the kind of enthusiasm that only an extreme morning person could muster.

Why was he not surprised?

He swung the door open and yawned.

"You said morning." She jammed one hand on her hip and held the other hand out, palm facing up. "Leash, please."

He glanced past her to try to figure out how she'd managed to breach the perimeter of the fence Jenna had slapped up between their opposing sides of the patio.

Ally followed his gaze and shrugged. "You left your door open."

He'd have to watch that next time he offered to let her walk his dog. Seriously, it was summertime. Weren't kids supposed to be sleeping in?

He held up a finger, signaling she should wait. Then he scooped a very sleepy, very confused Tank into his arms and clipped a blue leash to the dog's collar. Lucas couldn't remember the last time he'd walked Tank on a leash. Usually, his pup trotted around faithfully at his heels. But Ally seemed determined to do this properly, so he carried Tank back to the patio and set him gently on the ground.

"All right, I don't have any rules." Lucas handed the leash over to Ally. "Just bring him back when you're done."

She stared blankly at him, probably because she'd never encountered a rules-free experience. Her hand came to rest on Tank's head. "You sure you don't want to come with us?"

Lucas arched an eyebrow. "That would defeat the purpose of you walking my dog."

"Except you might have fun."

He considered it for a moment, then came to his senses. What was with his sudden interest in hanging out with kids? "Nah. I'm good. I should get back to my nap."

"Suit yourself." She wagged a finger at him as if taking a nap was criminal. It didn't take a genius to know where she'd learned that move.

Ally took a step, but Tank stayed put. He cast Lucas a glance, heavy on the puppy-dog eyes, as if he too expected Lucas to come along.

Not going to happen.

"Go on." He pointed at the stairs.

Tank shuffled after Ally.

Lucas yawned, grabbed the latest copy of his favorite surfing magazine and plopped down on the porch swing. He flipped through the pages, only half-seeing the print. He needed coffee—or some serious, uninterrupted shut-eye.

But sleep wasn't going to be possible because suddenly Ally's little dog walk had become much louder than he'd anticipated.

"Hurry up, Tank," she said from somewhere down below. "Tank, please."

Then, more desperately, "Come on, Tank."

The poor dog. Maybe Lucas should have gone along, after all. He tossed his magazine onto a nearby table and ambled over to the porch railing. A quick glance at the patch of sand at the foot of the stairs confirmed what he suspected—Ally's walk was a structured affair. She'd take a few steps and then order Tank to sit or lie down, neither of which was in his repertoire of dog tricks.

Ally looked exasperated. Tank looked... amused. Happier than Lucas would have guessed, albeit thoroughly confused.

Lucas laughed to himself. "Sorry, buddy. She's a task master."

Ally came by it honestly, though.

"Just like her mama," he muttered.

Ally returned from her walk with Tank brimming with excitement. She talked nonstop about the dog while she sat at the kitchen table and drew fanciful pictures of Tank with her favorite magic markers. His scruffy little face now peered at Jenna from the half dozen drawings Ally had tacked to the refrigerator with beach-themed magnets. All of a sudden, the kitchen looked like a canine art gallery.

As grateful as Jenna was to Lucas for letting her daughter borrow his dog, she needed to somehow distract Ally from her Tank obsession. Drastic measures were necessary. It was probably only a matter of time before Ally began begging for a dog of her own. Again.

Only one thing could do the trick: a trip to Ally's favorite island eatery, Ocean Burger.

Jenna piled the kids into the car and got to the popular restaurant early enough to snag a spot with a beautiful sea view. Ocean Burger was located right on the beach in a building painted bright pink with pretty lime-green and turquoise paper lanterns hanging from the rafters. From their table on the deck, they could see palm trees swaying in the breeze, the long stretch of Tybee's white sand beach, and foamy waves tumbling onto the shore.

Plus, the burgers were outstanding. Jenna dipped one of her fries into a dollop of ketchup as Nick and Ally peppered her with questions about her manuscript.

"I don't get it. She's learning to sail, but only so she can get to the lost island?" Nick's brow furrowed.

The lost island was a new idea for Jenna.

It hadn't appeared in her first book—hence Nick's confusion. Hopefully, he'd have a better grasp of her plot once she was finished with her manuscript and he could read it. If not, she was in more trouble than she realized.

She popped the fry into her mouth. "That's the idea. At least that's how I'm writing the first draft."

Ally took a sip of her lemonade, which was almost as pink as Ocean's Burger eye-catching exterior, then giggled. "And she's only eleven. So does that mean in two more years I can sail, too?"

Nice try. But there was no way in the world Jenna was going to let either one of her kids out on the open water alone. She wrote young adult fantasy novels—emphasis on *fantasy*. "It's just fiction, sweetie. Besides, she comes from a long line of sailors. Your grandparents came from Chicago. Two very different scenarios."

Nick's gaze narrowed. "So how does it end?"

Jenna wished she knew. "That's a good question."

"I thought it was due like, really soon." Ally looked at her like she was a kid who'd failed to do her part of a group project at school.

"Soon-ish." She still had a few weeks. Granted, her word count was on the meager side. She had whole chapters left to write, plus a read-through of the manuscript...not to mention the ending that she still hadn't quite figured out.

The anxious expressions on her kids' faces weren't helping matters.

Jenna forced a smile. "But I'm not worried, so you can't be worried."

Who was she kidding? She was definitely worried.

Why was she at Ocean Burger when she still had no clue how to finish her manuscript? The ending was a crucial part to any book. Some said it was the *most* crucial. Nothing ruined a good story like a bad ending.

Jenna's ending wasn't bad, it was nonexistent.

"Great." She reached for the bill. "Should we go home?"

Jenna was suddenly more than ready to get to back to her laptop. She just hoped that whatever activity Lucas and his carefree friends had going on was somewhat quiet. Or better yet, she hoped he was enjoying a nice, solitary afternoon.

Not that she cared if he was dating Kayla or any of the other slim, tanned, child-free twenty-somethings who had flocked to his bonfire the night before...

Except she sort of did care, which was

nearly as worrisome as the unfinished ending to her manuscript.

"That's it!" Lucas spiked a white ball over the net and fist-pumped as it landed in a spray of sand, just out of reach of the players on the other side.

After Ally returned Tank, he'd called a few friends and thrown together an impromptu beach volleyball game. He needed something to get his mind off the kids next door.

And their mother.

It wasn't like him to get involved like this. Even Kayla had noticed, and his response to her teasing kept whirling through his thoughts.

It's just one kid, just one time.

Suddenly one kid had become two, and he was starting to lose count of how many times he'd volunteered himself. He'd even managed to volunteer his *dog*. What was happening?

You like her. That's what's happening.

The ball sailed toward him and he pounded it with more force than was probably necessary. Being attracted to Jenna Turner was out of the question. She wasn't interested. Plus she was leaving in just a few weeks *and* she had two children.

He wasn't father-figure material. He'd pretty much organized his entire life to avoid that kind of responsibility.

The ball sailed past him, and when he turned to run after it, his gaze snagged on Jenna and her kids walking over the dune toward the beach house.

His favorite three complications.

Nick broke away from Jenna and Ally and ran toward him. Lucas gave him a wave. "Hey, bud."

The boy grinned toward the group scattered about on the makeshift volleyball court they'd marked in the sand. "Lucas, do you need any more players?"

No, they didn't. Certainly not a kid whose head probably didn't reach the bottom of the net.

"I guess we could use another body." What was he saying? "Why? You interested?"

Nick's grin widened. "What about my mom?"

Wait. What?

Lucas snuck a glance at Jenna standing in the distance, facing the ocean. She was wearing her emerald swimsuit again, this time under a beige sweater and jean shorts. Hair tossed by the sea breeze, she looked like a mermaid on her way to the library.

Lucas rather liked the library. And mermaids. "What about her?"

"She used to play in college." There was an unmistakable note of pride in Nick's tone.

"Really?" Lucas tried to keep his jaw from dropping. It was a struggle.

He called out to Jenna. "Hey, you used to dig?"

She came toward him, eyeing him like he was speaking a foreign language. "What do you mean?"

The kid had to be mistaken. She wasn't even familiar with basic volleyball jargon.

"I was just telling Lucas how you used to play volleyball in college," Nick said.

Lucas waited for her to contradict him.

She didn't. Not exactly, anyway. "That was like a hundred years ago."

Nick shrugged. "You should play."

"Right now?" She blinked.

Lucas bit back a smile. "Were you any good?"

Jenna crossed her arms and stood a little straighter. "Team captain."

Things were getting more interesting by the second. He stared at her sweater—so prim, so *beige*. "I'm having a hard time picturing that."

Her cheeks flared pink and she laughed. "Why? Because I'm wearing a cardigan?"

"That might be part of it." Plus he just couldn't picture her being into team sports, maybe because of the fence that divided his patio in half.

"You know what, let's go." She gathered her hair over one shoulder and started twisting it into a braid with nimble fingers. Clearly, she meant business.

Lucas tossed the ball back and forth from one hand to the other. "Let me guess. You want to be on my team?"

She rolled her eyes. "You and me. First to ten."

Was she serious? She'd just admitted she hadn't played in years.

"So this is a challenge?" He peered at her more closely.

A spark of defiance flashed in her gaze. "Oh yeah. And if I win, no music past nine o' clock. If you win, I won't complain about your little mid-week matches anymore."

Lucas glanced at Nick. A wager this serious needed a witness.

Nick nodded. Off came Jenna's cardigan.

So he wasn't just imagining things. Jenna Turner had actually just challenged him to a one-on-one volleyball war.

"You've got yourself a bet." He tossed the ball in the air and caught it in one hand without looking. "Show me what you've got."

The other players formed a curious circle around them, clapping and cheering when they realized Jenna had just thrown down the gauntlet. Lucas almost felt sorry for her. If she truly hadn't played ball in years, she didn't stand a chance. But this whole spectacle had been her idea, hadn't it?

He served the ball with a gentle smack, nice and easy. He didn't want to embarrass her, but he wasn't about to let her win. If a challenge was what she wanted, then that's what she'd get.

Jenna returned the serve with surprising force and it zipped right past him, eliciting a cheer from Nick and Ally. When Lucas turned to grin at them, he spotted Tank nestled happily between them. The furry little traitor.

Lucas chased after the ball and pitched it to Jenna since it was her turn to serve. He moved up a few steps, expecting it to barely clear the net.

Wrong move.

The ball sailed past him again. He dove for it and missed by a mile. Jenna was now up by two, and all Lucas had to show for his efforts was a face coated in sand.

"Eaten by the sand shark," she teased.

He couldn't help but laugh. Jenna was good. She was *really* good, and to top it off, she could trash-talk, too. Who would have known?

He got up and dusted himself off. "Is that all you've got?"

She bounced back and forth on the balls

of her feet and spread her arms out in the universal gesture for *bring it on.*

No more Mr. Nice Guy. Going easy on her had clearly been a mistake. The next time he hit the ball, he didn't hold back. They volleyed back and forth, back and forth, until Jenna's fingertips grazed the ball and it plunked to the ground. A very near miss, but Lucas was finally on the board.

The longer they played, the closer the score got. The advantage seemed to flip with every serve. As soon as Lucas was up, Jenna would win a point and vice versa.

The crowd surrounding the court multiplied and every time one of them missed a volley, they broke out into cheers. Lucas was pretty sure most of them were rooting for Jenna now.

When he won the next point, he show-boated a little, bowing to the spectators. Tank let out a howl. Lucas couldn't remember the last time he'd had so much fun playing volleyball. He also couldn't remember the last time he'd been on the losing side of the net.

She wasn't actually going to beat him, was she?

Miss Team Captain called out to him, all business. "Nine all. Match point."

The volley that followed was their longest back-and-forth yet. Lucas gave it his all, but in the end, he ended up flat on his back in the sand.

The ball bounced past him, and Jenna fist-pumped like she'd just won gold at the Olympics. "Yes!"

She'd won fair and square. Lucas wasn't even mad about it. More than anything, he was impressed.

And maybe just a little bit captivated.

Seeing Jenna so happy and carefree made him overly aware of his own heartbeat. His mouth went dry, and he wasn't altogether convinced it had anything to do with exerting himself for the past half hour.

Ally and Nick ran toward Jenna, and she scooped them off of their feet and into her arms. Tank yipped and ran circles around them. Lucas might as well have been invisible to his own dog.

He peeled himself off the ground as his friends offered him consolatory pats on the back. People were talking to him, but he barely heard a word. All of his attention was focused on the victor, smiling from ear to ear on the other side of the court.

"I guess we've got a new rule," she said as he bent to cross under the net.

"I guess so." No more music past nine o'clock. What was he supposed to do at night now instead of practicing his guitar? Sip chamomile tea on the patio and watch the moon shimmer over the ocean?

That sounded kind of nice, actually. Although it would have been nicer without a barrier keeping him away from his neighbor, who suddenly seemed full of surprises.

He raked a hand through his hair and came away with a fistful of sand.

Smooth. Real smooth.

Why was he nervous all of a sudden? It wasn't like he wanted to impress her.

"Good game, man." She flashed him one last grin and threw an arm around each of her kids. "Come on, let's go."

Nick beamed at her. "Great job."

"Thanks. I had my good-luck charms." Jenna gave Ally and Nick's shoulders a squeeze as they made their way toward the beach house.

Lucas watched them until they disappeared over the dunes, and even though he was still surrounded by friends, he noticed a twinge of something that felt almost like sadness deep in his chest. It wasn't until he thought about Jenna's crazy fence again that he recognized the feeling for what it was.

Loneliness.

Chapter Seven

T HE FOLLOWING MORNING, LUCAS PULLED his Jeep into a small parking lot off Main Street, climbed out and held the door open for Tank. The pup hopped down from the driver's seat and trotted to the front door of Lucas's favorite island bookshop. Lucas being a creature of habit, Tank knew the drill. He let out a squeaky dog yawn as he waited patiently for Lucas to catch up with him.

"Sorry to keep you waiting." Lucas scratched him gently behind his ears.

Tank's tail wagged, beating the backs of Lucas's leg when he pulled the door open.

"Good boy, bud," he said.

Tank loved coming on errands. He especially loved the bookshop because it was a newsstand, book store and coffee shop all in one. During the winter months—when All the tourists went back to their regular year-round lives and Tybee all but shut down—

Lucas liked to spend long mornings here, drinking coffee with his head in a book and Tank curled at his feet.

Bells chimed on the door as they entered, announcing their arrival. Sandy, the full-time bookshop owner and newbie barista, looked up and greeted them with a smile.

"Lucas, hi!" Her gaze shifted lower. "And hello there, Mr. Tank. Can I interest you in a doggie treat?"

Tank bolted from Lucas's side, gently plucked a sizable bone-shaped biscuit from Sandy's fingertips and dragged it to the fiction section.

"Would you like some coffee?" Sandy ran a dishrag over her pristine espresso machine. "A latte or cappuccino perhaps?"

Lucas glanced around the quiet shop. During the summertime, late mornings like this one were pretty quiet while families hit the beach. In the early dawn hours, it was the busiest place on the island's south end.

"Who's manning the machine?" He nodded toward the fancy piece of equipment.

Sandy had been so proud to have it installed. She vowed it would "elevate the coffee scene" on Tybee, and she'd been right. The only trouble was that she still hadn't mastered its fancy operating system. So long as one of her part-time baristas was on the scene, everything was fine. But with Sandy at the controls, plain coffee was definitely the best option.

"It's all me today. I sent Josh home about a half hour ago." She flipped a switch on the espresso machine and steam came out of one of its openings.

Odds were it was the wrong one, but Lucas didn't want to hurt her feelings. He pasted on a smile. "A cappuccino sounds great."

Sandy's face lit up, and Lucas couldn't help but wonder if he'd been the first taker in the fancy coffee department since Josh had left. "Coming right up."

"Thanks." He glanced at the sludge coming out of the machine and promptly averted his gaze. "Listen, I was wondering if you could help me with something else."

"Anything." The older woman nodded. "Although, if you're looking for surf magazines, I'm plum out. I can hardly keep them in stock this time of year."

"No, thanks. I'm good." He cleared his throat and looked around, just in case Jenna or one of her kids happened to be lurking behind a bookshelf somewhere. That Ally, in particular, was a stealthy one. "I'm looking for a book."

"Any book in particular?"

He nodded. "Yes, a young adult fiction book by an author named Jenna Turner? I'm not sure what it's called, but I think it's the first book in a series."

Curiosity had gotten the best of Lucas, and he'd Googled Jenna after their fateful volleyball match. He couldn't help it. Her ace volleyball skills had him searching for information about her sports background, but as soon as he'd typed her name into the search engine, dozens of hits popped up about her literary career. Apparently, her debut book had been a smash hit. Book bloggers and readers were anxiously awaiting her sequel, which he assumed must be the book she spent all her spare hours working on back at the house.

He wasn't sure what had compelled him to make the trip down here in search of her first book. Logic told him he simply wanted to give it a read because it had garnered such praise online. But he was beginning to realize that logic didn't come into play much where his feelings for Jenna were concerned. Not that he had *feelings* for her, per se. Of course he didn't. She was impossible with a capital I.

At the same time, he wanted to know more about her. He was particularly curious about her writing. Until he'd stumbled upon all the articles about her book, he'd honestly assumed she'd been joking when she told him she wrote teen fiction. Weren't fiction writers supposed to have artistic tempera-

ments? Obviously not. Judging by her personality, he would have guessed she wrote
textbooks. Or computer manuals, maybe.

"Oh, of course we have that one." Sandy
pushed a giant cup of steaming something
that in no way resembled a cappuccino
across the counter toward him. "That author's book was a bestseller, hugely popular
with the tween crowd. The sequel is supposed to come out next year sometime. You
just enjoy your coffee while I go find it for
you."

A smile tugged at Lucas's lips. So Jenna
was a well-known, bestselling author? Well,
how about that.

The "cappuccino" was predictably terrible, but he dutifully choked it down while
Sandy stepped over Tank and searched the
shelves for Jenna's name. Relief washed over
him when she located the book and carried it
back to the counter.

"Found it." She handed it to him and
took her place behind the cash register.
"Anything else I can get you?"

He clutched the book to his chest with
one hand and dug out his wallet from his
pocket with the other. "No, this is it for now.
But thank you."

Sandy ran his debit card and handed it
back to him. "I have to say, I can't remember
you reading YA before. Usually it's surf mag-

azines, local history or books about nature. Why the sudden interest in the fantastical adventures of a teen sailor?"

Tank looked up from his biscuit, ears pricked forward. He could be a nosy little thing.

Lucas glanced down at the book and flipped it over in his hand. Jenna's photo looked up at him from the back of the dust jacket.

"I guess sometimes tastes change," he said by way of explanation.

So much for logic.

Much to Jenna's relief, Lucas was true to his word and honored the results of their wager. There wasn't a volleyball in sight after she dropped off Nick and Ally at summer camp the following morning. Lucas's Jeep wasn't parked in its usual spot in the driveway, but he pulled up in the drive shortly after she got back and slipped quietly into his side of the house with Tank trotting happily behind him.

The scene on the opposite side of the fence had been strangely silent ever since— not that Jenna was complaining. She simply wondered what Lucas was up to, and then she reminded herself it was none of her business. She needed to take advantage of the peace and quiet while it lasted. The view off the duplex was as tranquil as a beach sounds relaxation app.

Strong cup of coffee in hand, Jenna tucked herself into one of the Adirondack chairs on the lower level of the patio and got to work. She pored over the pages she'd written so far and tried her best to come up with the perfect ending to her book. Despite the soothing surroundings, it just wasn't happening.

What was she going to do?

Maybe I should just make the main character get lost at sea. The End. Then I wouldn't have to figure out how to deal with any of these plot holes.

Somehow she didn't think that would appeal to readers. Plus it felt like cheating. Also, she needed to earn her advance, so setting metaphorical fire to her book and walking away wasn't an option. There had to be a way to end her story with a shiny red bow that would make everyone happy—her readers, her editor and most of all, her publisher, Stan. Because if Stan wasn't happy, her newly successful career as an author just might be over.

She stared so hard at the typewritten pages, willing an ending to materialize, that she almost didn't hear her cell phone's ringtone as it chimed from somewhere beneath her pile of papers and writing books.

"Shoot, shoot, shoot! Where are you?" Coffee cup abandoned, she dug around until she found the phone buried beneath a throw pillow decorated with sea turtles. "Gotcha."

A knot of dread formed in the pit of her stomach as she peered at the name on the tiny screen: Stan.

Oh, boy.

Could his timing be any worse? Yes. Yes, it could, because just as she was about to answer the call, Lucas appeared mere feet away on the opposite side of the fence.

She nearly dropped the phone. "Oh, wow. You're always right there, aren't you?"

He shrugged one shoulder. "I suppose you could've built a higher fence."

Touché. "Believe me, I thought about it."

She couldn't have this conversation with Lucas so nearby. He was so...*distracting.* Surely he'd leave once she answered the phone.

"Hello?" She swallowed. Stan said something, and Jenna was only vaguely aware of what it was. Lucas still stood there on the other side of the fence. Why wasn't he going anywhere?

She darted toward the staircase. "Hi, how are you? Yeah, I'm just running upstairs."

As she fled, Stan asked if she was just about finished with her manuscript.

Jenna nodded. "Am I almost done with

the draft? Absolutely. It's practically writing itself."

Except for one minor detail—the ending.

Luckily, he didn't press for more information. Instead, he launched into a detailed explanation of the publicity plan for her upcoming book. The marketing department was so convinced it would be a huge hit that her initial print run would be nearly double the size of the first printing of her debut book. She should've been thrilled. Every author dreamed of this kind of support, but as happy as the news made her, it also made her deadline feel more pressing than ever.

Only three more weeks!

Guilt tugged at Jenna's conscience as Stan began to heap praise on her, but then she stopped listening to him because she caught sight of Lucas down below, leaning against the fence and reading a stack of papers that looked an awful lot like her manuscript. She froze.

No.

He wouldn't.

But, oh yes. He would.

Her gaze darted to the arm of her Adirondack chair, and sure enough, her pages were no longer where she'd left them. She aimed her fiercest glare at Lucas, which he didn't notice at all. Instead, to her complete and utter horror, he picked up her red pen and began making notes in the margins of her manuscript.

What. In. The. World.

"Hey. Hey, hey!" Jenna leaned over the balcony, waving frantically at him. He ignored her, but of course Stan thought she was talking to him. "What? No, sorry. I was just saying *hey*, I should probably finish that ending."

She managed to get off the phone as quickly as she could. "Excellent, bye."

Excellent? What a joke. Nothing was excellent—not her non-existent ending and certainly not the fact that Lucas was downstairs critiquing her manuscript. It wasn't ready for anyone to see yet. She hadn't even let her kids read it, much less a perfect stranger.

Although Lucas wasn't exactly a stranger anymore, was he? He was almost beginning to feel like a friend...

Or at least he *had* been until he'd stolen her pages.

"Would you stop reading that?" She flew down the stairs and lunged across the white picket fence, but he gathered the manuscript close to his chest and leapt out of reach.

"I have to admit, I really love this Jasmine character. But this yachtsman, he's a little stiff for my taste." He made another red mark in the margin.

Unbelievable. "Are you seriously giving me notes right now?"

"What? A surfer can't have a literary opinion?" He frowned as if he was the injured party.

"I didn't say that," she countered.

He pointed at her with the pen. "Yes, but you thought it."

Okay, so maybe she had. But it wasn't as if she'd seen any bookshelves in his bachelor pad on the one occasion she'd ventured across the fence.

Besides, he was the one in the wrong here. It wasn't even a contest. "And you thought it was okay to just reach over and grab it?"

"All I'm saying is that the sailors I know are just normal people who love sailing." He gestured to her typewritten words, which were beginning to seem more and more ridiculous the more Lucas spoke. "They don't run around wearing brass buttoned jackets and ridiculous..."

She did *not* need this right now. Her confidence was shaky enough as it was.

"Okay, we're done here." She snatched the pages from his hands. "Thank you very much."

"Besides that mess of a character, I think you've got yourself a really good story." He leaned against the picket fence and grinned at her.

How was it possible for someone to be

so incredibly frustrating and yet charming at the same time? It was a lethal combination.

She scowled at him. "You're impossible, you know that?"

"What? I'm giving you a compliment." His dimples flashed, and Jenna thought about reaching across the fence to strangle him.

Instead, she turned on her heel and walked away. Why hadn't she seen this coming? He'd been arrogant from the start, which is exactly why she'd built the fence to begin with. Yet somehow, she'd actually started to like him, despite her every effort not to.

"You're welcome," he called after her.

She turned to glare at him one last time, but her heart gave a foolish tug at the sight of those dimples again.

And that's when Jenna realized just how much trouble she was in where Lucas McKinnon was concerned.

Jenna stomped through the sand on her afternoon beach walk with Maureen the next day, brimming with furious adrenaline.

The more she thought about Lucas reading her manuscript without her permission, the angrier she got. Who did he think he was, with his darling dog and his flirty dimples and his *literal* boy-next-door charm? Maybe, just maybe, she didn't dislike him quite as much as she had when they'd first moved into the duplex, but did that give him the right to pore over her pages?

No, it did not.

He'd even made red notes all over the margins. It was a *first draft*. First drafts were always sort of terrible, which was exactly why she hadn't let anyone look at it yet.

The worst thing about his scribbled red notes—the *very* worst thing—was that his comments were surprisingly insightful. He'd honed in on all the problem areas, and after going through his notes, she'd actually come up with a kernel of an idea for an ending. At last.

If it had been anyone else, she might have been thrilled, perhaps even grateful. But it hadn't been anyone else. It had been *him*.

"It's like a total invasion of privacy, am I right?" She threw her arms in the air and waited for Maureen to agree with her, but her friend suddenly wasn't walking beside her anymore.

"Do you think you could slow down?" Maureen said.

"That's the problem, I can't. Not even a little bit because I'm already like fifty pages behind, and my neighbor is so not helping. *At all.*" Jenna's tongue was moving even faster than her footsteps.

She passed the lifeguard stand and continued her rant. "Every time I sit down to work, bam! He's right there. He's like that annoying insurance commercial that's on every time you turn on the TV."

Somewhere behind her, Jenna heard wheezing.

"Maureen?" Jenna turned around and found her friend standing completely still with her hands on her hips, gasping for breath. "Are you okay?"

"I think I missed that last bit." Maureen was so far behind her that her words were nearly swallowed up by the crash of the waves on the shore.

Jenna backtracked and shot her friend an *I'm sorry* grimace. "See, I'm out here, not even close to the house, and he's still driving me nuts."

It crossed her mind that maybe she couldn't realistically blame Lucas for the fact that she'd left Maureen behind and nearly speed-walked right off the end of the island, but she didn't care. She was ready to blame everything on her neighbor at the moment— bad weather, her aching calf muscle, all of it.

"Well, if you guys are anything like my seventh graders, you taunt the ones you like." Maureen sounded so calm. So rational.

It was maddening. "I love you, but no. That's not it."

The corners of Maureen's mouth turned up. "Maybe?"

"I promise you, this is *not* some middle school crush. He doesn't even like me." He certainly didn't like the way she characterized sailors. And he seemed to have a special disdain for her cardigan. "He's just...impossible."

Maureen's gaze narrowed. "Maybe I was talking about you."

"What? No, I don't...I *can't*." She couldn't possibly have a *crush* on Mr. Slack.

Just...

Absolutely not.

"I can't be distracted." She took a deep breath. "So, *no*."

"Okay," Maureen said, although Jenna wasn't sure she believed her. "Then what are you going to do about it?"

"I don't know." Honestly, she'd already built a fence. What else could she possibly do to keep Lucas McKinnon out of her life? *And out of my thoughts, as well.* "Check my blood pressure two times a day?"

Maureen rolled her eyes.

Jenna sighed. "Okay, maybe three."

"I'm sorry, but you're going to have to come up with a better plan than that."

"Right. A plan." Jenna took off down the beach again. She always thought better when she was moving.

Maureen trudged behind her. "That still seems fast."

Maybe she didn't need to think quite so hard. Jenna slowed her steps before she accidentally walked all the way back to Savannah.

Going back home didn't sound so bad all of a sudden. She'd never do that to Nick and Ally, though. They loved being at Tybee.

But that didn't necessarily mean they needed to continue living within inches of Lucas McKinnon, and Jenna knew precisely how to make that happen.

The second she returned to the beach house, she flipped through the welcome book the rental company had left on the picnic table on the upper deck. It was filled with instructions for things like trash pickup and recycling, along with menus for local restaurants and take-out pizza. It also listed the rental company's phone number right on the first page.

Jenna tapped the number into her cell phone and held her breath while it rang on the other end. "Please answer, please answer. Please…"

A recorded voice picked up. "You've reached LM Management. Sorry we can't take your call. Please leave a message at the tone."

Jenna debated whether or not to hang up. Maybe she should.

It's now or never.

She walked to the deck's wooden railing and glanced down at the wholly ineffectual picket fence stretching from one end of the patio to the other and decided she was doing the right thing. Lucas had left her no choice.

As soon as the tone sounded, she launched into her request. "Hi. This is Jenna Turner at your Seawatch property. I hate to do this, but I was wondering if we could change rentals?"

She paused when she heard barking down below. The last thing she needed was for Lucas to overhear her message.

But when she took another peek at the patio, he wasn't anywhere to be seen. Just Tank, yipping happily on his way inside the house.

"The location is perfect, and the property is really sweet, but our neighbor..." The words stuck in Jenna's throat. Why was this so hard all of a sudden?

And why did it seem like she could hear her words echoing from Lucas's open windows?

The phone lines must be acting up, or maybe she was only imagining things. She took a steadying inhale. "I mean, it's one thing to live next door to a stubborn messy surfer when you're single, but when you're a single parent with two young kids you can't have distractions day and night. And I've got a lot of work to do, so..."

Words failed her again. Seeing Tank's wagging tail and jaunty trot had thrown her off her game. The pup was her Achilles heel where Lucas was concerned. He loved that dog like a child. It was the most endearing thing about him.

She squeezed her eyes shut and tried not to think about his scruffy little face or the way Lucas talked to the dog like he was his actual best friend. "I'm sorry. I'm rambling. But if you have anything, please let me know. Please?"

Chapter Eight

LUCAS SHOWED UP EARLY FOR summer camp the following day. *Too* early. Every so often, Kayla ran the kiddos through track and field events out on the beach before swim practice. Nick was busy racing Grayson in a mad dash on the sand, and from the looks of things, he fared a good bit better on land than he did in water.

Lucas hung back at a distance and watched. Outside of the pool, Nick was like a completely different kid—brimming with confidence. So confident that he even engaged in some good-natured trash talking.

"You ready for this sandstorm?" Nick grinned at Grayson in the lane beside him as they struck starting poses.

"My feet won't even touch the ground," Grayson said.

Kayla let loose with her whistle, and Nick and Grayson took off barefoot down the beach alongside eight other kids. The two boys pulled easily into the lead while the other campers clapped and cheered.

Interesting.

All Lucas needed to do now was figure out how to tap into that easy self-assurance when Nick was in the water. There had to be a way.

Before he could formulate a plan, one of the kids standing and cheering on the sidelines of the footrace broke away from the group and sprinted toward him, arms waving wildly. "Lucas!"

He knew at once it was Ally. She had more intensity in her little finger than all the other children on Tybee combined.

"Hey there, you," he said when she came to a stop in a flurry of sand.

"Here." She dug something out of the pocket of her pink shorts. "I made this for Tank."

Lucas stared at the thing dangling from her fingertips. It looked as if she'd scooped up every shell she could find and strung them together with bright blue nylon.

"What is it?" He wasn't actually sure he wanted to know the answer.

"It's a collar."

Oh, boy.

"Well. You know, it's very..." Lucas struggled for the right word. "...decorative."

"It's not decorative. It's to help him stop

pulling." Ally gave the collar a little yank as a demonstration.

"Oh, okay. Now I see. That is..." *Outrageously optimistic.* "...very smart of you."

"I know," she said, so sure of herself. *Just like her mom.*

Was it crazy that Lucas found the mother-daughter resemblance kind of adorable?

"Nick helped, too." Ally tucked her hair behind her ear with her free hand and rolled her eyes. "And he hates crafts."

Lucas laughed. Just as he suspected, Nick was a kid after his own heart. "Then that's very sweet. Of the both of you."

She shoved the collar closer toward him, dangling it mere inches from his face.

He stifled a laugh. "Oh. It's even pretty close up."

"Will you give it to him?"

The odds of getting Tank to actually wear the thing were miniscule.

Still, Lucas couldn't help but feel touched. He'd never been on the receiving end of a homemade gift from a child before.

He swallowed hard and took the collar, holding it close to his chest. "You know what, he's going to love this."

Ally beamed at him and took off skipping back toward the other campers.

"Thank you," he called after her.

It looked like the campers would be busy

on the beach for another hour or two, so Lucas went home to present Tank with his new collar. The dog accepted the gift with a wary sniff, but once Lucas fastened it around his neck, he changed his tune. His tail wagged, and he even seemed to have a little extra spring in his step. Either that, or Lucas was losing it.

Probably the latter. The surf report called for ideal conditions today, and he hadn't gone anywhere near his board. Even more mystifying, he wasn't at all tempted to skip swim practice at the summer camp to catch a few waves. Nick was relying on him, and watching him race on the beach had given Lucas a few ideas.

Back at camp, he watched Nick make another half-hearted attempt to swim a lap. Just like the day before, he ran out of steam midway across the pool. When at last he popped his head out of the water and grabbed onto the concrete lip of the pool deck, Lucas knelt down to greet him.

"You can't tell me you're not competitive. I saw you running around out there." He nodded toward the beach where the orange cones had been set up for the field events.

Nick brushed water from his eyes. "It's not the same thing. We always race."

"You should want to push yourself the

same way here." Lucas tapped a finger on the deck.

"I do," Nick countered.

Lucas shrugged. "Then I'm going to need to see it."

"I thought we were done." Nick glanced toward the other campers climbing out of the pool and toweling off.

"Do you want to improve your time or what?" Lucas pointed to the other side of the pool. "Go!"

Nick took a deep breath and launched himself back into a freestyle stroke in the opposite direction.

"Go, go, go!" Lucas slapped the water for extra encouragement, then he stood so he could get a good look at Nick's form.

He was definitely going a little faster this time. Lucas gripped his stopwatch tighter, as if he could will the kid to make 1:18. Right as he neared the halfway point, Kayla walked past Lucas.

He looked up from the stopwatch just in time to catch her smirk, paired with a meaningful glance. "What?"

"Nothing." Her smirk intensified. "I'm just saying…"

She made little mouse ears with her hands—another Disneyland reference.

"Cute. Really cute." It was never going to happen. "And *no*."

She laughed and kept walking while Lucas turned his attention back to Nick's stroke. He finished just shy of his goal time, but instead of climbing out of the pool, he took off again without prompting from Lucas.

Back and forth he went. Every time Nick glanced at Lucas, he would stretch his arms overhead, demonstrating long, reaching strokes.

"Come on, reach for it. One more time." He pushed the button on the stopwatch again.

Nick's form was getting better and better. His slender arms were now stretched to their maximum length, and he was reaching farther out, extending his stroke from his shoulders. Instead of staying flat, facing the bottom of the pool, his body pivoted slightly with each flip of his arms, weaving through the water with greater ease. Even his kick was looking more efficient.

Something in Lucas's chest blossomed and swelled. He couldn't stand still, so instead he began pacing up and down the length of the pool alongside Nick. "You got it. Good form. Come on."

The moment Nick's hand touched the pool wall, Lucas pushed the button on the stopwatch and grinned.

Not bad. At last, we're getting somewhere. Nick shot him a hopeful look from behind his swim goggles. "Did I get it? What's my time?"

Lucas took a backward step, giving the kid room to climb out of the water. After all that effort, he'd earned a break. He'd just swum his best time yet, but before Lucas could give him the good news, he collided with something behind him.

Except it wasn't a some*thing*. It was a some*one*.

Lucas closed his eyes.

No. It couldn't be her...not now. Could it?

Sure enough, when he opened his eyes, Jenna stood glaring at him with her arms crossed and her brow furrowed. Lucas thought about shoving the stopwatch into his pocket and feigning innocence, but somehow he didn't think that would fool anyone, least of all the most conscientious mother on the planet.

"You're early," Nick stammered.

Busted.

No matter how hard she tried, Jenna couldn't believe what she was seeing. Lucas...child-averse *Lucas McKinnon* was at the summer camp pool, and it seemed as if he was acting as Nick's personal swim coach.

Was she in an alternative universe or something? Never in a million years would she have expected Lucas to go out of his way to help her son. Yes, he'd been letting Ally walk Tank every morning lately. But this was different.

So different.

Coaching required time and effort. It required commitment, and Jenna was fairly certain Lucas didn't know the meaning of the word.

Yet here he was with a whistle around his neck and a stopwatch in his hand. It was utterly confusing.

And kind of...sweet. Endearing, even.

At least it would have been if anyone had bothered telling her it was happening.

She narrowed her gaze at Nick as he climbed out of the pool. *Really?* This wasn't like him. Jenna and her kids didn't keep secrets from each other. She'd always been especially proud of the close relationship she had with Nick and Ally. They talked about everything. She thought they had, anyway.

Nick sloshed his way to the nearby bleachers and sat down. He couldn't seem to look at her as he toweled off and slid his feet into his flipflops. Jenna didn't know whether to feel angry or heartbroken.

Lucas's continual presence wasn't helping matters.

"I think I should probably leave you guys to it," he finally said.

"That's probably a good idea." She tried to smile but it wobbled off her face.

She kept her arms crossed as he walked away. *Keep it together*. Hadn't she already made enough of a spectacle of herself in front of him, what with the fence and everything?

Lucas took a seat on the bleachers on the opposite side of the pool, as if they were members of opposing swim teams. For some reason, the thought made Jenna feel even worse—as did the tender expression on Lucas's face every time he glanced at Nick.

Lucas didn't even like kids—at least that's what he'd implied since the day she'd moved into the duplex. The affection in his eyes while he'd been grinning down at that stopwatch said otherwise, though.

She took a deep breath and sat down beside Nick. Trying to stand while she processed what she'd just seen simply wasn't possible. "I don't get it. We tell each other everything."

Nick cast a wistful glance at Lucas. "I know you don't like him."

"Maybe as a neighbor, but this is different." This wasn't about distractions or noise or Tank jumping in the middle of her work.

This was about Lucas helping her kid...

Even after she'd built a literal barrier to keep him away.

But it was also about Nick lying to her. They'd *both* lied to her.

"He's a good coach, Mom. I mean, he's not my coach but he's been helping," Nick said.

"That's not the point."

"And my time is improving. Slowly." He gave her a hopeful grin, and somewhere beneath the guilt in his expression she saw something else there.

Pride.

Warmth coursed through her. It had been a long time since Nick had felt good about his swimming. Not making the team last year had crushed him.

"I'm glad, bud. I am. It's just..." Why hadn't he told her Lucas was helping him?

She swallowed. She knew exactly why he'd kept it a secret. This was all her fault.

Nick gazed up at her. "I'm sorry."

She wrapped an arm around him and pulled him close. "Let's get your sister. We can talk about this more when we're home. Okay?"

"Okay."

Jenna looked over the top of Nick's head, toward Ally leaning against the snack counter and chatting with her camp friends. "Come on, Ally. Let's go."

Ally waved goodbye to the other kids and hurried toward the bleachers.

"Grab your stuff, okay?" Jenna said.

While Nick and Ally gathered their things, she couldn't help noticing that Lucas was still sitting on other side of the pool—watching, waiting, although Jenna wasn't sure what for.

All she knew was that she had the sudden feeling that maybe there was more to the surfer next door than she wanted to admit.

Lucas knew he'd screwed up.

He'd known all along that keeping the swim lessons from Jenna was a mistake, just like he'd known that he wasn't exactly her favorite person. But he'd underestimated exactly how much she'd disliked him, apparently.

There was no denying it anymore, though. She loathed him. Why else would she want to pick up her kids and move?

He stared at his answering machine, grinding his teeth as her message played aloud.

I mean, it's one thing to live next door to a stubborn messy surfer when you're single, but when you're a single parent with two young kids you can't have distractions day and night. And I've got a lot of work to do, so...

Lucas had already listened to the message three times. He wasn't sure why he was playing it again. Obviously, she didn't realize that the LM in LM Management stood for Lucas McKinnon. That was probably his fault, too. He'd failed to mention that significant detail. They'd gotten off to such a rocky start and pointing out that he owned the place almost felt like it would be pulling rank on her. She'd been so flustered when she'd lectured him about houseplants and ground rules. If he'd told her right then that he was the person cashing her rental check, she would have pulled her cardigan over her head and never shown her face again.

Lucas didn't want that. Jenna had a lovely face...and even though she thought he was messy and stubborn, he wanted to see more of it. Every now and then, he thought the feeling might even be mutual and she just didn't want to admit it. Clearly, that wasn't the case.

I'm sorry. I'm rambling. But if you have anything, please let me know. Please?

Jenna wanted to leave the beach house. She couldn't even tolerate him for five short weeks.

Lucas sighed. He didn't like the idea of Jenna and her kids packing up and moving. He didn't like it at all. Before he could figure out what to do, a knock sounded on his front door. He got up and dragged himself to the patio where, lo and behold, Jenna stood on the other side of his screen.

He started defending himself before he even let her in. He simply couldn't help it. "All right, I get why you're mad. I just don't see what being messy has to do with it."

Her brow crumpled in confusion. "I'm sorry?"

"Fine," he relented. "You're right about one thing."

She blinked. "I haven't said anything."

He leaned against the doorjamb and studied her through the screen. Funny, she didn't look nearly as anxious to move out as she'd sounded on the answering machine.

Did she really not know what he was talking about?

Impossible. She probably wanted to hear him admit how very wrong he'd been.

"We should've told you we were having lessons." There. He'd said it. "But I was just trying to help the poor kid out."

"I know." Her voice softened.

Something inside Lucas softened too. "You know?"

Had they just *agreed*?

"That's why I'm here." She held up a gift bag. Lucas had been so ready for an argument that he hadn't noticed it dangling from her fingertips. "Can I come in?"

"Yeah." His breath caught. "Of course."

He held the screen door open for her, and she stepped onto his side of the patio. It felt monumental, like trumpets should sound or something.

"Thanks." She glanced around, wide-eyed, as if she was as surprised as he was by the sudden turn of events.

"Whatcha got there?" He pointed at the gift bag.

He was acutely unsure of what to do with his hands. Or where to stand. Or what to say.

"A little thank you," she said.

A spark passed through his fingertips as she handed him the bag. What was wrong with him all of a sudden?

She shrugged. "Don't let the color fool you, they're actually pretty good."

Lucas reached into the bag and pulled out a Rice Krispies treat that looked like it might contain a box of melted crayons.

It was the least appetizing, most wonderful thing Lucas had ever seen. "You made me dessert?"

"The kids picked the flavor." Jenna smiled. Until now, Lucas hadn't realized *rainbow* was a flavor. "I just wanted to let you know how much I appreciate what you've been doing for Nick."

She wasn't angry at him anymore. On

the contrary, she was being kind to him... kinder than he deserved.

His throat grew thick. "I'm really not doing much."

Jenna shook her head. "That's not what he said."

"Well, then he's being very generous. I'm just helping him out when I can. It's nothing." Lucas inspected the Rice Krispies treat in his hand so he wouldn't have to see the tenderness in Jenna's gaze. As nice as it felt to suddenly find himself on her good side, it was also confusing.

Probably because he liked it more than he should have.

"Maybe." She shrugged. "Or maybe you care a little bit more than you want anyone to know."

Busted...

Again.

Her lips curved into the softest of smiles. "Either way, I hope you enjoy the treats."

He held up one of the colorful squares as if it was a trophy. "Are you kidding? Rainbow-colored food is my favorite type of food."

"Okay. I guess they know you better than I do." She laughed, and then she looked at him in a way that made him feel like she was seeing him for the very first time.

An intimate silence settled between them, and Lucas finally caught a glimpse of what it might be like to finally be on the same side as Jenna Turner. Warm. Nice. Like a perfect day at the beach.

"So." She lifted her chin. What was going on in that head of hers? Whatever it was, Lucas hoped it didn't have anything to do with his lack of houseplants. "You'll keep me in the loop?"

He nodded. "I will now."

"Great. Thanks." She gave him one last smile before slipping past him back to her half of the deck. "Good night."

"Good night."

After she'd gone, he stood alone in the moonlight for a long moment, turning the colorful Rice Krispies treat over in his hand.

"I guess they're staying," he whispered, and then he took a bite.

A truce—however temporary—had never tasted so sweet.

Chapter Nine

$\mathcal{J}$ENNA JUGGLED HER CAR KEYS, three
tote bags and her purse as she attempted to corral Nick and Ally down
the bright white steps of the deck the next
day. Parenting was a balancing act— sometimes metaphorically, and other times, quite
literally.

She hadn't been doing such a great job
in the parenting department lately. Yesterday
had been a prime example of that fact. But
today was a new day. She'd apologized to Lucas for judging him when all along he'd been
going out of his way to help Nick. Ally too,
if all the hands-on dog experience counted,
which it most definitely did.

The apology had gone rather well, actually. Much better than she expected. He'd
been so sweet. Humble, even. Jenna didn't
sleep much afterward. Every time she closed
her eyes, she saw Lucas smiling his crooked
smile and holding onto that ridiculous Rice

Krispies treat as if it were something to be treasured.

Sometime around five in the morning, she'd given up on sleep and attacked her manuscript with renewed vigor. Lucas's notes had been surprisingly insightful, and by the time the kids had gotten up, she'd managed to write ten new pages—good pages. She'd written more while they'd been away at camp, so now they were celebrating with a trip to the park for Tybee's regular Thursday night outdoor concert.

If she could stop thinking about Lucas and that silly Rice Krispies treat long enough to get Nick and Ally in the car.

"I'm king of the mountain!" Ally shouted as she stomped down the stairs, reminding Jenna that she was supposed to be *parenting* instead of romanticizing a marshmallow cereal snack.

Lucas was her neighbor. Nothing more.

"You can't be king." Nick whizzed past Ally.

Ally still managed to beat him to the bottom step. "Why? Because I'm a girl?"

"No, because *I'm* king!"

They continued battling back and forth on their way to the van, which didn't bode well for the drive to the park.

Jenna took a deep breath. "Okay, you're

both kings. Now, everyone in their seats. We're supposed to be there in ten minutes."

As soon as she reached the gravel drive, Lucas's voice boomed from the upper deck. "Keep it down out here. I'm trying to sleep."

She glanced up at him as she tossed the tote bags into the trunk. "It's five o'clock in the afternoon."

His dimples flashed. "I was kidding. That was a joke."

"Oh, were you pretending to be me?" Jenna's cheeks went warm. "Ha. Very funny."

She slammed the trunk closed.

"I try." Lucas leaned against the porch railing. Something had definitely shifted between them. Apparently, they were neighbors who chatted and joked around now.

Jenna didn't hate it.

She may have even loved it a little bit.

"Are you guys heading to the concert in the park?" Lucas said.

Jenna shot a purposeful glance at Ally and Nick's heads poking up from the top of the sun roof, where they watched her interaction with Lucas with far too much interest. "If everybody will get in their seats, yes."

Nick stayed put, grinning at Lucas. "Are you coming too?"

Lucas nodded. "Every Thursday."

Of course, whereas most Thursday nights back in Savannah, Jenna attended PTA meetings or made homemade cupcakes for the monthly school bake sale.

"Lucky," Ally said in a singsong voice.

"Why don't I drive you?" Lucas nodded toward his Jeep, parked beside the van.

Jenna froze.

So now they were the sort of neighbors who rode to concerts in the park together? It felt too much like a date.

She knew it wasn't. *Obviously.* But still...

The thought of riding together made her feel jittery and nervous for reasons she didn't want to contemplate, so she seized upon the first excuse she could find.

"You want us to ride in *that*?" She pointed at the Jeep.

The vehicle didn't even have a roof. Plus the entire backseat was occupied by one of his many surfboards. It was a legitimate concern.

"Mmm-hmm." Lucas nodded.

"Cool! Can we?" Ally and Nick begged in unison. "Please?"

"I mean, does that thing even have seat belts?" Jenna countered.

But she knew when she was outnumbered.

Minutes later, she was sitting beside Lucas in the front seat of the Jeep as they crossed the island bridge toward the park. Tank was tucked in between Nick and Ally in the back, wearing the seashell collar the kids had made him a few days ago. Jenna felt uncharacteristically wild and carefree. A sea breeze whipped through the Jeep, tossing her hair and her thoughts into a whirl.

I was right. This doesn't feel like a date. It feels more like...a family.

"This is awesome," Ally said, shouting above the wind.

"Okay, this is pretty cool." Jenna's smile was so wide that her cheeks ached.

And then she remembered the night of Lucas's bonfire and all the young, pretty girls whose smiles had been just as bright—most notably Kayla. She'd taken Jenna's place beside Lucas as if she belonged there, and every time Jenna saw them together, she couldn't help but wonder if they'd ever dated.

Meanwhile, five minutes in Lucas's Jeep had her fantasizing about a happy, beachy family life. Maybe she needed to build a fence around her daydreams instead of the patio.

"Not as bad as you thought?" Lucas grinned at her from the driver's seat.

Her heart did a foolish little tumble. "No. Not bad at all."

She almost wished she could say otherwise.

For as long as Lucas had lived at Tybee, pretty much everyone on the small barrier island gathered in Memorial Park on Thursday nights for free concerts.

Every week, a different band from one

of the surrounding cities in Georgia took the stage while concert-goers lounged in the grass on blankets. Beneath the dramatic limbs of the oak trees, they snacked on items from the surrounding food trucks and swayed to and fro to the music. As fun as it was, it didn't really seem like Jenna's thing. Then again, he hadn't thought volleyball was her thing either, and he'd been wrong about that.

As she sat beside him in the Jeep, grinning from ear to ear, he came to a profound realization. Despite all her rules and regulations, Jenna Turner was full of surprises.

He smiled quietly to himself as he pulled into the gravel lot beside the park. Lucas rather liked surprises.

They piled out of the Jeep and headed toward the picnic area. Lucas had never come to a summer concert with an entourage before—certainly not an entourage that included children. He wasn't sure whether he should sit with his neighborly trio or go his own separate way. After all, it wasn't a *date*. He'd simply given them a ride.

But Nick remained glued to his side, even when he paused to let Tank sniff a few trees. The kid was obviously starting to look up to him, which should have been his cue to cut and run. He was completely out of his depth. Maybe if his own dad had ever taken him to the park when he was Nick's age, he'd know what to do or how to act.

Strangely enough, though, Lucas didn't mind Nick's admiration. Maybe it had something to do with the bag of Rice Krispies Treats Lucas polished off with his coffee earlier this morning.

Maybe it also has something to do with Nick's mother.

"So do you think you might have time for another lesson?" Nick said.

The question was a welcome distraction from the dangerous trajectory of his thoughts. He could sense mouse ears looming in the periphery.

"Under one condition." Lucas held up a finger. "No hugging."

According to Kayla, that was the tipping point.

"I don't get it." Nick's eyebrows scrunched together. "Why would I..."

Before he could press for an explanation on the no-hugging condition, the mouse ear expert herself turned up.

"Hi." She gave Lucas a friendly hug.

"Kayla, hello. How are you?" Out of the corner of his eye, Lucas spotted Nick hustling to catch up with Ally and Jenna. Maybe he'd do the same, now that he'd set some boundaries.

He swallowed. Gosh, he was beginning to sound like someone he knew.

"I'm good," Kayla said.

"Would you do me a favor? Will you take Tank?" Lucas offered her Tank's leash.

She took it. "Absolutely."

"Thank you." The odds of finding some space on Jenna's blanket would probably be easier without Tank cruising for crumbs. Besides, the dog loved Kayla. Ally had been taking up so much of Tank's time that he hadn't seen much of her lately.

"I'll catch you in a bit, okay?" Lucas waved, and as he walked away he could have sworn Tank winked at him.

Lucas might be doing a half-decent job of fooling himself where his affection for Jenna's kids were concerned, but his dog clearly had his number.

Jenna found Maureen and Ian on a large patchwork quilt smack in the center of the grassy picnic area. She tightened her grip on her tote bags as she drew near, acutely aware of her tardiness.

Not that a picnic was a structured sort of affair. But Jenna was never late—not for social engagements and definitely not with her book deadlines. A flicker of worry passed through her at the thought of her book, but she reminded herself of all the amazing progress she'd made since the night before and she breathed a little easier. She still had a couple weeks. Everything was under control.

Except, oh yeah, she was late for the concert because she'd been riding around in an open-air beach vehicle with her handsome neighbor.

"Hey, guys." She dropped her belongings at the edge of the quilt and attempted an apologetic smile.

It was no use. She wasn't sorry. Not one bit. Riding in Lucas's Jeep had been fun. Her hair was probably three times bigger than it had been when she left the house, but she didn't even care.

"Hey," Ian said.

Maureen's gaze narrowed. She looked at Jenna like she no longer recognized her. "For someone who's so punctual, you're really late."

"Sorry, we decided to ride-share." Jenna sat, hoping against hope Maureen wouldn't press for details.

But of course she did. "You decided to what?"

At that precise moment, Lucas strolled into view and Maureen's features brightened with understanding.

"Oh, right." She beamed at him while Ian bit back a knowing smile. "Hey, neighbor."

Lucas hovered at the edge of their cozy set-up. "Surprised to see me?"

Always one for directness, Maureen nodded. "Maybe."

"Does this mean we need to make more room?" Ian aimed a pointed glance at Jenna. "Or build another fence?"

She laughed. Fine, she deserved a little teasing about the fence. It had been an impulsive, and ultimately disastrous, idea.

"Make more room. Right, Lucas?" Maureen nudged a wicker picnic basket off to the side.

Jenna should probably put a stop to things before Maureen physically dragged him onto the blanket. Because again, they were *not* on a date. The ride in the Jeep was basically a glorified Uber trip.

Was it, though?

"Actually, I think Lucas is meeting his girlfriend. So we should let him…"

Lucas plopped onto the quilt as if he belonged there. "My what?"

Seriously? He was going to make her spell it out for him when he'd just been hugging Kayla mere feet away?

"Um." Why was the back of her neck suddenly so warm? "Your girlfriend."

Lucas's response was a blank stare. "Who's that?"

Jenna glanced at Kayla walking Tank

beneath the shade of a row of Southern live oaks. Mercifully, he followed her gaze so she wouldn't have to say any more.

"Kayla? Oh, no. I've known her for years." Lucas shook his head. "She's like a little sister to me."

"So, she's not your girlfriend?" Maureen's eyebrows rose.

Real subtle, Maureen. Jenna's neck was on the verge of bursting into flames.

Beside her, Lucas was as cool as a cucumber. As per usual. "Nope. She's *definitely* not my girlfriend. Just a good friend that I happen to employ."

Jenna's embarrassment over her friend's overt attempt at matchmaking took an immediate backseat to her astonishment.

"What do you mean *employ?*" She blinked. "At the summer camp?"

Lucas shrugged. "I guess technically you could call it *my* summer camp, but I've never been one for job titles."

Then he winked at her, and Jenna longed for the ground to open up and swallow her whole. All this time she'd been thinking of him as Mr. Slack when in reality he owned the summer camp where her kids had been going every day for weeks. Why hadn't he told her?

Probably because you didn't give him a chance.

"You are definitely joining us." Maureen dug a frosted bottle of water from the nearby ice chest and handed it to Lucas, her business-owner neighbor.

"Absolutely," Ian said.

"Thank you." Lucas opened the water and took a sip. Jenna noticed that Ian's expression had turned wistful. Could he be thinking, like she was, about how much he'd enjoyed camp as a kid?

Lucas nodded. "Yeah, I feel pretty lucky. I mean, to be able to make a living doing this."

"So you actually *own* the summer camp. And that's why you're always there?" Maureen's gaze flitted toward Jenna. The words *two-week rule* were written all over her face.

"I also like the free food at the snack bar, so there's that." Lucas laughed.

He was being such a good sport about the interrogation. Even so, Jenna was still trying to wrap her head around the idea of Lucas as an entrepreneur. The summer camp had a definite beach vibe, so it sort of made sense. But his next bit of news was too much to comprehend.

"Before I moved here and opened up the summer camp, I worked at an investment banking firm. A normal work week included fifty-plus hours behind a desk and zero time outdoors, much less surfing. Two years in, I realized it was always going to be that way, so I decided to throw my corporate plan out the window and build the sort of life I wanted. I came up with a plan to give the new generation a real appreciation for the shore and keep them busy during the summer, both things I find a lot more meaningful than crunching numbers." He grinned. "Plus now I have plenty of time to surf."

It had to be the most drastic professional transformation story Jenna had ever heard. She narrowed her gaze, trying to imagine him screaming into a cell phone and running around in a suit—both of which her ex-husband did on a regular basis. "You really did the whole corporate thing?" Lucas McKinnon didn't belong in a coat and tie. Maybe he was joking.

But he wasn't. He was completely and utterly serious. "For a while. To save up some money for the camp. Luckily, I made some good investments."

"No." Jenna couldn't stop shaking her head. "I can't believe it. I'm shocked."

"Which part?" He leaned closer. "That I own the place, or that I actually have a 'schedule?'"

She could practically see the air quotes hanging around his last word. "Nick mentioned that?"

The corner of Lucas's mouth tugged into a half grin. "He sure did."

"Kids are like parrots," Maureen said in her teacher-of-the-year voice. "They'll repeat everything you say."

Ian nodded. "Oh, yeah."

"He must have taken it out of context," Jenna said, but she stumbled over her words.

"It's not a big deal. Hey, I would've assumed I was unemployed too." He raised an eyebrow and she laughed.

She also did her best to ignore Maureen and Ian's curious glances. Not an easy task when the two of them were clearly under the impression Lucas was flirting with her.

Was he flirting with her?

"You're funny," she said.

Lucas's smile faded, replaced with an earnestness that made Jenna's heart skip a beat. "How's that?"

"I don't know. I just can't figure you out." There, she'd admitted it. Everything she thought she knew about Lucas was wrong. She wasn't sure what to think anymore, except that she might actually like him. A lot.

He shrugged one shoulder. "What can I say? I'm full of surprises."

Then his gaze fixed with hers for a long, breathless moment, and Jenna forgot all about her noise complaints and Tank jumping in the middle of her manuscript and Lucas's lack of houseplants. She even forgot about the nagging reality of her book deadline. Every bit of her awareness was centered on Lucas's dark eyes and how very alive she felt when he looked at her like that—like he really saw her. Not just as a mom or an author or an obsessive control-freak of a neighbor, but as a woman. No one had looked at her that way in a very long time.

Lucas was full of surprises indeed.

And they kept on coming. After they'd listened to the band for a while and eaten a few of Maureen's legendary pimento cheese sandwiches, Lucas joined Nick, Ally and Grayson for a game of catch. He tossed the ball with the kids while Tank leapt in the air, trying his hardest to get a bite out of the football.

Jenna kept trying to remember how she'd come to believe that he didn't like children. He was a natural. She felt like she'd been spending the past few weeks with her head buried in Tybee's fine white sand.

"See. He's not such a bad guy once you get to know him," Kayla said as she stepped beside Jenna in line for ice cream at one of the food trucks lining the park.

"Oh, hi." Jenna looked away from Lucas, but apparently it was too late. She'd already been caught watching him play with the kids. "No, I didn't think he was a bad guy."

Did the entire island know about the fence? Terrific.

"No?" Kayla's forehead creased. She'd *definitely* heard about the fence.

"Okay, I wasn't a huge fan at first. But he's been really amazing to my kids, so there you go." Across the grassy field, Tank yipped and ran circles around Lucas as he caught a wobbly toss from Nick. Jenna cleared her throat. "I actually thought you two were together."

"Please. I'm so not his type." Kayla let out a laugh. "And he's not mine."

"Really? Because I think you're everybody's type." Kayla was lovely. And kind. And young. Sometimes Jenna felt one hundred years old around her.

Maybe it was the cardigan.

But Jenna liked her cardigan. Just like she enjoyed staying home with a good book or playing board games with her kids. It was simply who she was.

"We're just good friends." Kayla shook her head.

"That's good. I mean, either way would've been good. But..." *Stop talking.* If she kept stammering like this, Maureen wouldn't be the only one who thought she had a crush on her neighbor. "...good."

Kayla started to say something, but before she could get it out, the ice cream guy asked for her order. They'd reached the front of the line.

"Can I get the lemon sherbet, please?" Kayla said.

Jenna breathed a sigh of relief. Talking to Kayla about Lucas made her profoundly uncomfortable.

But Kayla wasn't finished. She turned back to Jenna while she waited for her order. "Can I just give you a friendly warning?"

"That sounds ominous."

"He's a sweet guy, for sure. But a family man he is not." She sighed. "He likes his freedom way too much."

It shouldn't have come as a surprise. Kayla's words confirmed everything Jenna already knew.

Still, they hurt.

"Then I guess it's good I'm not looking for anything." She pasted on a smile.

"You sure about that?"

Am I?

Of course she was sure. Yes, Lucas was charming. And yes, he was pretty great with her kids. He might not be Mr. Slack, but he was still a surfer who lived at the beach year-round and she was a suburban mom who packed lunches and organized carpool. What little free time she had was spent writing, and somehow she was still always behind.

Besides, she wasn't ready for a relationship. She might *never* be ready.

"Yeah. I've already been disappointed by

one relationship. I'm not trying for another." She couldn't survive another divorce. She'd rather be single for the rest of her life than be blindsided like that again.

Jenna nodded toward the ice cream truck. "I think your sherbet is ready."

"Thank you." Kayla took her order and dug into it with a spoon. "Bye."

"Bye." Jenna waved before turning her attention to the menu, grateful to be thinking about something as simple as ice cream flavors. "How about two vanillas and one strawberry sorbet?"

The sorbet was for Ally. Nick's favorite was mint chocolate chip, but the ice cream truck's selection wasn't quite that vast. Jenna always chose vanilla. She liked her ice cream simple and classic.

But as her gaze strayed back toward Lucas and the kids, she couldn't help wondering if maybe choosing something new every now and then might not be such a bad idea.

Chapter Ten

NICK NEEDED A BREAK FROM the pool.

Lucas took one look at him the following day at camp and knew the poor kid had hit a wall. He'd been practicing so much that his arms hung at his sides limp as spaghetti noodles. Swimming laps in his exhausted state would be fruitless. His times were bound to be slower, which meant Lucas would have a very frustrated child on his hands at the end of the day.

But the lessons didn't have to stop entirely.

He shot Jenna a quick text message asking if it was okay to take Nick on a quick outing away from camp. He had, after all, promised to keep her in the loop. She agreed right away and thanked him for checking with her first.

Lucas grinned to himself. Progress.

Then, when the other campers lined up poolside to swim their afternoon laps, he handed Nick a bike helmet and told him to put on a t-shirt and shoes and meet him in the parking lot. He aired up the tires in two of the camp's cruiser bikes and had them cleaned up and ready to go by the time Nick joined him on the gravel drive.

Lucas straddled his bike, waited for Nick to fasten the strap of his helmet, and then pushed off toward the northwest end of the island.

They peddled in silence, side by side, as Lucas led them off the main road toward the bike path that ran along the island's old historic trail. Sand crabs skittered across the dusty track, and they could hear the splish-splash of dolphins playing in the nearby river channel. Nick grinned when he spotted a pair of them cresting in the distance.

It wasn't until the Cockspur Island light-house came into view just offshore that Nick got curious enough to press Lucas for some information. "I probably shouldn't ask this, but why are we here and not at the pool?"

Lucas slowed his bike to a stop as they rolled from the path onto the loose sand of the beach.

"You see that out there?" he said, pulling off his helmet.

Nick climbed off his bicycle and squinted at the horizon. "The old lighthouse?"

"Yeah." Lucas raked a hand through his

helmet-hair. "That old lighthouse is how I got over my fear of swimming."

Nick laughed. "Oh, please. You were never afraid."

"You're right." Lucas nodded. "I was terrified."

Nick took off his helmet and stared at him. The kid apparently thought he was Aquaman. "Of what?"

"The open water." The sea and the mysteries of what hid in its depths had scared the life out of him when he was a boy. Every time a piece of kelp touched his foot, he'd been convinced it was a shark. "That's not great when all you want to do is surf. So I told myself if I could swim to that lighthouse and back again, I'd drop the whole scared stuff."

Nick studied the lighthouse's worn exterior. Originally built on an oyster bed, it had been part of Tybee's landscape since the mid-eighteen-hundreds.

"How old were you?" he finally said.

"I don't know." Lucas thought about it for a second while a seagull swooped low in front of them. "Probably about your age."

Nick's eyes went wide. "Oh, great. So now you want me to swim out there too? To improve my time?"

"No, definitely not." The channel wasn't

deep, but it had a powerful current. "In hindsight, it wasn't the most logical plan."

It had been pretty reckless, actually. He hadn't brought Nick to the lighthouse to teach him anything about swimming. He wanted to try and change the way the kid thought.

Nick sighed.

"Look," Lucas said, "I'm not worried about your swim trials. I know you're going to hit your time." He was within a fraction of a second of 1:18 already. "All I'm trying to say is, it's pretty amazing how strong you can be if you're pushed to it."

He paused before adding, "Even if you have to push yourself."

Because the truth of the matter was that Lucas wouldn't always be there cheering Nick on. When he went to school swim try-outs in the fall, he'd have to make it across the pool on his own. If he could teach the boy anything, it would be to push for the things he cared about. Things he loved. But maybe that wasn't a lesson he could impart so easily. He and Nick were running out of time together.

Thinking about it made Lucas feel oddly hollow inside, and he'd been thinking about it quite a bit lately.

"Wow. That was kind of deep," Nick said.

"Don't get used to it, kid. Deep is boring." Lucas used to think so, anyway. But he was beginning to have a whole new perspective on the things that made life interesting.

Lucas shot a quick glance at Nick and reached for his helmet. He'd said what he needed to say. It was time to stop thinking about the end of summer and enjoy the moment for what it was. The sun was high in the sky, and back at camp there was a hot dog with his name on it. "You hungry?"

"Yeah, sure." Nick swung a leg over the seat of his bike.

"I'll race you to lunch." Lucas waggled his eyebrows, hoping to stoke some of the competitive fire he'd seen when Nick raced Grayson on field day.

It worked.

Nick pumped hard on his petals, zipping past him and leaving a ribbony trail in the sand.

"You're on."

At long last, Jenna was closing in on the end of her manuscript. Over the past few days, she'd written a detailed outline for her final chapters plus an epilogue. Now all she had to do was finish getting the words she'd planned so carefully onto the page before her deadline, which was now less than two and a half weeks away.

Thankfully, Nick and Ally had both been

in bed since eight-thirty. They'd both been so exhausted after another day at summer camp that they'd fallen asleep on the couch during family movie night. Even a bowl of popcorn sprinkled liberally with mini-chocolate chips couldn't keep Ally awake.

Jenna had been banging away on her laptop for over an hour at the kitchen table, but just as she was hitting her stride, the sleepy silence of the beach house was interrupted by music drifting through its walls. Jenna's fingertips paused over her keyboard. She heard voices above the beat of the music—loud, cheery voices.

Was Lucas having a party?

She glanced at the time display on her cell phone. It read 10:05 p.m.

"Okaay."

His party, or whatever he had going on over there, was in clear violation of the 9 p.m. rule that had been established after her volleyball victory. She'd earned that victory, and she'd had the sore biceps for days to prove it.

Maybe she should cut him some slack, though. He'd been so great with the kids lately.

She started typing another sentence, but before she got to the period at the end, the music cranked up a notch. Jenna glared at the wall separating her half of the house from Lucas's. When she glanced back down at her computer screen, she'd forgotten what she'd been trying to say.

Great. She was going to have to go over there, wasn't she?

Never mind the fact that she was once again going to come across like a major wet blanket, but now she'd have the added humiliation of busting up a party to which she wasn't invited. She and Lucas were friends now. She'd thought they were, anyway.

Right. And you're just the sort of party animal he'd want at one of his bachelor bashes.

It didn't matter. She had work to do, and it was a full hour past the noise curfew.

She pushed back from the table and slipped out of the house as quietly as she could so she wouldn't wake Nick and Ally. As soon as she stepped out onto the deck, she could see silhouettes of people milling around Lucas's side of the duplex. Ten or fifteen, at least.

His door was wide open, so she waltzed inside without bothering to knock. Jenna realized a second too late that even though she was wearing a plain blue t-shirt, it was paired with her favorite shorty pajama bottoms. Not exactly festive attire.

Oh well.

No one seemed to register her presence anyway. The lights were dim, and a crowd was gathered on Lucas's sectional sofa—

Tank included, of course. Nearly everyone balanced a laptop or tablet on their lap, and the huge flat screen on the wall was paused on a still of a swimmer doing the backstroke. EPSN, maybe.

What was this? A fantasy water sports league?

Jenna crossed her arms. "Are you really having a party on a Tuesday?"

On the far end of the sofa, Lucas looked up from his computer and flashed a smile, giving her the full-on dimples treatment. "Are we really being that loud?"

She looked around and spied another small group of people in the kitchen. Soda bottles and pizza boxes littered the counter.

Jenna sighed. Pepperoni sounded delicious right about now, but that was beside the point. "I don't want to be a killjoy, but—"

"It's nice to see you," Lucas said.

Tank let out a woof of agreement.

"Don't try to charm your way out of this one." She wagged a finger at both of them. "I won the bet, fair and square."

"Oh, so you think I'm charming?" His mouth twitched. The guy sitting beside him stopped typing and shot a curious glance at Jenna.

"What?" She blinked. "No."

Maybe just a little bit, especially when he

and his dog were tag-teaming her like that. She was only human.

"You sure?" He cocked his head, and of course Jenna noticed that it was a handsome head. Very handsome indeed.

Again, a completely irrelevant observation.

Tank let out a snort. Super. Even the dog knew she was lying.

Her face burned with embarrassment. She knew coming over here was a terrible idea. "Stop trying to change the subject."

"It isn't a party."

"No?" She gestured to the people around her. "What is it, a 'hang out?'"

Lucas typed for a second and then stopped. "We're working."

"You're *working*?" Ha. Jenna was a parent. She knew loafing off when she saw it.

"Well, that guy over in the corner isn't." Lucas tipped his head toward a bearded man carrying a fresh tower of pizza boxes. "But everyone else is. We just wrapped a little promotional video."

The guy next to him, who was now following their interaction with rapt interest, shook his head. "It's not that little. Some dude wants to franchise the summer camp."

"Someone wants to invest? Like a *Shark Tank* guy?" Jenna asked.

Every now and then, her penchant for reality television came in handy.

Lucas tapped a few more keys on his laptop. "Actually, an old classmate of mine from Berkeley. He comes down next week so it's crunch time."

"Wait." Jenna must have misheard. "You went to UC Berkeley?"

"Just for my MBA," he said as if Berkeley wasn't one of the top MBA schools in the country.

Mr. Slack not only owned a summer camp and was an experienced businessman, but he also had a graduate degree. And now he was about to be a beach camp mogul of some sort. Had she ever been more wrong about a person in her life?

"Hence the two-week rule," she muttered to herself.

Maureen would never let her live this down.

"What's that?" Lucas glanced up from his screen again.

Jenna envied his concentration. Maybe he'd learned how to tune out distractions at Berkeley. "Nothing. You're obviously busy, so I'm going to get going."

She turned to head back to her pizza-less side of the duplex where writer's block and a vague sense of shame probably awaited her.

She'd jumped to conclusions about Lucas. Yet again.

He stopped her before she got to the door. "Jenna?"

"Yes?" She turned to find him smiling at her again.

"We'll keep it down."

"Thank you." He really was a good guy. "You really are full of surprises."

Chapter Eleven

HE FOLLOWING WEEKEND, MAUREEN INVITED Ally and Nick to bowling night and a sleepover for Grayson's birthday. For Jenna, the evening couldn't come soon enough. Thanks to several extremely late nights, she'd finally finished the first draft of her manuscript. She still needed to do a final read-through, but the only things on her agenda while the kids were away were dinner for one and a long, luxurious bubble bath.

"Did you guys remember your socks?" she asked as she helped Nick and Ally get settled beside Grayson in the backseat of Maureen and Ian's SUV.

Ally held up her favorite pair of pink crew socks. They had glittery gold threads running through them. "You can't bowl without them."

"Unless you want foot fungus." Nick giggled while Grayson pulled a face.

"Yeah, I think we get the idea, bud," Jenna said. Maybe she'd gone a little overboard on her lecture about why socks were such an important part of a good bowling wardrobe. "Have fun! And happy birthday, Grayson."

"Thanks, Ms. T." Grayson grinned.

Jenna could hardly believe he was already turning twelve. Before she knew it, Nick and Ally would be off to college and she'd be...

Alone.

Best not to think about that now, though. She had a tub full of bubbles upstairs with her name on it. Besides, there was nothing wrong with living alone.

And anyway, she was years away from empty-nest syndrome.

Still, the thought of Maureen and Ian taking the kids bowling together made her feel suddenly wistful. She loved being a mom, but every now and then she missed being part of a couple too.

Lucas's lopsided boy-next-door smile flashed in Jenna's mind, and she blinked. Hard.

Maureen frowned at her from the driver's seat. "You better relax. It's your one night off."

Jenna nodded. "I will."

Had Lucas been right? Does she even know *how* to relax?

Of course you do. The bubble bath, re-member?

Did she really like bubble baths, though? She honestly had no idea. She normally barely had time to shower, much less soak in the tub.

Maureen narrowed her gaze. Why did Jenna get the feeling she too didn't believe Jenna knew how to relax? "You promise?"

"Swear." Jenna held up her hand as if she were taking an oath.

Maureen nodded and shifted the car into drive. "Okay."

Jenna backed up to give them plenty of space to pull away. "Drive safe."

She waved until Maureen's car disappeared from sight. Then she took a deep breath.

She could do this. Totally. What kind of person didn't know how to chill out?

Tank barked from the opposite side of the patio fence.

Don't answer that, pup.

So much relaxation was about to go down. Jenna would relax all night, even if it made her miserable. But as she climbed the steps toward the deck, her stomach growled. Her pancake breakfast had been hours ago, and she'd been so busy getting the kids packed up for their sleepover that she'd skipped lunch.

First things first. She'd make a nice dinner for herself and *then* she'd relax.

Last night's supper had been meatloaf, and there was just enough leftover ground beef for a nice sized burger. Jenna put it on a plate along with a slice of cheese and headed out to the patio to fire up the grill. Because as everyone knew, grilling during the summertime was fun. It probably even counted as relaxation.

But when she flipped the switch of the gas grill, nothing happened.

"Oh, come on. Really?"

She tried a few more times, just to be sure. It was no use, thought. The grill refused to light.

Jenna sighed and looked longingly at Lucas's shiny silver grill on the other side of the fence. Tank immediately started barking. What was with that dog? It was almost like he could read her mind.

She was definitely thinking about sneaking to the other side of the patio and borrowing the grill. Lucas wasn't home, and after all, he'd reached over to her side and stolen her manuscript without permission. He owed her one.

Plus he'd never have to know.

She picked up the plate, but before she could take a step toward frenemy territory,

Lucas called from inside the house, "Tank, come eat."

So much for being sneaky.

Jenna put the plate down and sighed. When had he come home? "Hello? Lucas?"

Several seconds passed before he finally stepped outside.

"I'm sorry." He closed the door behind him. "I can barely hear you over that fence."

Very funny. "It never gets old, does it?"

"Nope." He planted his hands on the wooden divider and grinned.

Fence jokes aside, he looked almost happy to see her.

Jenna's stomach fluttered...which she attributed to hunger. She cleared her throat. "I was wondering if maybe I could use your barbecue. I just have this one thing."

Instead of answering her, Lucas glanced around. "Where are the kids?"

"Birthday party."

"Ah, lucky you," he said.

"Yeah." She nodded. Although so far, the relaxing thing wasn't panning out so well.

"You don't outsource much, do you?" He crossed his arms, and Jenna found herself staring at his forearms. They were nice—lean and sun kissed. Probably from all the surfing.

When she met his gaze again, his eyes seemed to darken a shade.

"Not usually, no." She shook her head. "It's actually kind of nice to have the night off."

"And that's what you're eating?" He aimed a sardonic glance at her raw hamburger.

It wasn't that bad, was it? "I was going to put cheese on it."

"That's pitiful." He shook his head and turned back toward his door.

So...what? He wasn't going to let her use his grill because he didn't approve of her plain-Jane dinner?

She opened her mouth to protest, but before she could say anything, he glanced over his shoulder. "Grab your cardigan."

The plate nearly slipped from her hand.

"Why?" She tightened her grip on the china and squared her shoulders. "Are you taking me out?"

Weeks ago, she would have recoiled at the idea. Now it sounded nice. More than nice, if she was really being honest.

Her heart beat hard in her chest while she waited for his answer.

"Maybe." He gave her a crooked smile and then disappeared into his side of the house.

Jenna's heart leaped. This was definitely better than a bubble bath. Or a fresh-grilled hamburger—even one with cheese.

She looked down at the modest meal on her plate and shrugged. "It's not that bad."

But somehow she knew that having dinner with Lucas would be even better.

Lucas wasn't about to let Jenna eat that pathetic little hamburger patty on her one night off of mommy duty. She deserved a night out, so he took her to his favorite place to eat on the island.

Located on an old, weathered pier that stretched far out over the ocean, Sam's wasn't exactly fancy. But it was special. Sam's had the freshest seafood in Georgia. It was practically a Tybee institution.

"This place never gets old. Even with all the crazy tourists, I just love it here." He turned and snuck a glance at her walking beside him as they made their way down the pier. "I can't believe you've been coming here four years in a row and you've never been to Sam's?"

"Not that I remember," she said.

Her hair was gathered over one shoulder, and she'd taken him at his word and slipped into a cardigan—a different one than she'd worn the day of their head-to-head volleyball challenge. That one had been the color of oatmeal cookies. This one was a deep sea blue.

He wondered how many of those cozy-looking things she had. He also wondered when he'd started to like them so much.

"Oh, you'd remember. This is the best food you're going to have in town." Lucas nodded at the man behind the walk-up counter as they approached the tiny yellow bungalow at the end of the pier. "Isn't that right, Sam?"

"Lucas!" The older man's face split into a wide grin.

It had only been a few days since Lucas had seen him last, but he'd never brought a date here before. He wasn't altogether sure he and Jenna were on a real date, but he liked to think so. "How's it going?"

"Good, if you're hungry. We got an early bite." Sam nodded toward the chalkboard where he always listed the daily catch in bright letters.

Lucas angled his head toward Jenna. "This is as fresh as it gets. What are you feeling like?"

"Um. I don't know. I eat everything."

Somehow he didn't believe her. "Girl after my own heart."

Her forehead crinkled. "Except cucumbers. People say they don't taste like anything, but they totally permeate. Even if it just touches a leaf."

There was the highly opinionated woman he knew…and liked.

A lot, as it turned out.

"If you're trying to get me to revise my previous statement, it's not going to work," he teased.

She smiled. "Then I eat everything."

Lucas laughed and ordered both items on the specials board. They could share. "How about you give us a whole crab, some of your garlic shrimp, two rolls and a big stack of napkins."

"Coming up." Sam's gaze flitted back and forth between Lucas and Jenna, and a smile tipped his lips.

"Thank you." Jenna's voice was infused with warmth, and suddenly their feud and especially their fence seemed a million miles away.

Jenna gave the crab in their basket a few ineffective whacks with the little wooden mallet Sam had given them. A pile of wadded napkins sat to her left and Lucas sat to her right, grinning at her attempts to break into the crab's shell.

She laughed. "I bet you take all your neighbors here."

He snorted. "Only the impossible ones."

"Oooh, I'm flattered," she teased.

But truthfully, she was. Even though their dinner was a spontaneous jaunt and not a date, it sort of felt like one, especially when Sam had looked at them as if they were a couple.

And now Lucas was looking at her in almost the same way.

It threw a her a little...in a good way. Although it was awfully difficult to crack open a crab when her hands were shaking.

She set down the mallet and watched Lucas's hands as he deftly peeled their mountain of shrimp. "I've gone through like fifty napkins already and you haven't used one."

He smiled and reached into the basket. "The trick is, you need to know how to grab the crab. See, first you take off all the legs and you hope to get some meat."

The shell made a cracking noise and he peered inside. "No dice. Okay, and then..."

The crab suddenly broke in half, spraying Jenna with a stream of melted butter. Lucas's eyes grew wide, and then they both dissolved into laugher.

"I think I need another napkin," Jenna managed to say.

He nudged a pile toward her. "You can have the whole stack."

She dabbed at her damp shirt, while Lucas finished peeling the shrimp without making any mess whatsoever. "When did you suddenly become the neat one?"

"Now you sound like Ally. She just says it like it is." His eyes lit up. "It's impressive."

"She really likes you. They both do." *So do I.*

She held her breath while he took in her words, hoping he knew just how much Nick and Ally's opinion meant to her. They were protective of her, in a way. And they'd certainly never taken to anyone quite the way they both had with Lucas.

But that was her fault, mostly. Since the divorce, they'd been their own little club, like the Three Musketeers. She'd been so willing to put her future on the line when it came to her writing, but her heart was another matter entirely. She'd barely dated at all.

Sitting by the ocean with Lucas made her feel different, though. She almost felt ready to give dating a chance.

"They have impeccable taste," he said softly.

He *knew.* He had to. She could see it in his eyes—he knew how much her kids adored him, and he didn't mind. In fact, it seemed as if he might adore them too.

She smiled from the inside out. Then she eyed the troublesome crab and shook her head. "Okay, you know what? I think I'm done with this guy, but it was delicious."

"Best in town." Lucas popped a shrimp into his mouth.

"Yeah." Jenna sipped her wine. The sun was beginning to set, casting pink and gold shimmering light over the ocean. At the end of Sam's long pier, they had a perfect front row seat.

She glanced sideways at Lucas. "You ready for your big meeting?"

He nodded as he watched the flow of the tide. "I think as long as I get a good surf in, I'll be fine."

Jenna still had a hard time picturing him sitting behind a desk at an investment banking firm. She couldn't imagine him anywhere but here, with his feet in the sand and salt on his eyelashes.

"Do you have a tie?" she said.

His expression sobered. "Do I need a tie?"

"You said they're pretty corporate."

He seemed to think about it for a second and then shrugged. "I'm not worried."

Jenna marveled at him. "Are you always this relaxed?"

"I figure as long as I've done the best I can on my end, I can let the rest go." He glanced at the ocean, and the sun dipping below the horizon, splashing the waves with light.

She followed his gaze and sighed. "I wish I could do that."

He angled his head toward her. "Let things go?"

"Stop trying to control things from all sides." Because that's what she did, wasn't it? She'd reacted to her divorce by trying to keep everything in her life so neat and orderly that she always knew what to expect.

Which left no room for nice surprises, such as the man sitting next to her.

"Well, you've got a few more sides to deal with than I do." His voice went low and uncharacteristically serious. "And you're killing it, by the way."

"'Killing it?' You think so?" Could he not see that beneath the rules, the noise curfew and her neatly alphabetized bookshelf, she was kind of a neurotic mess? "Because I don't even have an ending for my book."

"Isn't that normal for writers?" he said.

"I don't know. This is only my second novel. I mean, what if I only had one good one in me?" It was one of her worst fears, and she wasn't sure she'd ever said it out loud before. She always put on a brave face because she didn't want Ally and Nick to worry. About anything.

"Hey," he mock-scolded her. "Don't sell yourself short. Look at everything you're doing. Working from home, raising two kids."

He made her sound like Wonder Woman...in a cardigan. "Their dad is actually really helpful when he's not traveling."

His eyes narrowed. "You're still friends?"

"Friendship was never really our problem." Jenna and her ex had always gotten along. They still did. He'd simply woken up one day and decided he didn't want to be married anymore. "He wasn't home much. He was very into his career, but at the same time didn't understand why I wanted to be an author. I don't think he considered it a real job. We just had very different views on life. I wish I had figured that out sooner."

Lucas's smile turned tender. "But then you wouldn't be here."

And here wasn't such a bad place to be. It was pretty amazing, actually. "That...is very true."

"Don't worry, I have a feeling that your sequel is going to be even better than your first."

Were they still talking about her book? Because is felt more like they were talking about her life.

A shiver coursed through her. She couldn't tell if it was due to the gentle ocean breeze or the company.

"Here." Lucas gathered his jacket off the back of the bench where they were sitting and offered it to her.

"That's okay. I'm fine." She wrapped her sweater tighter around her frame.

"I know you're fine, but I'd still like to

give it to you. If that's okay?" His expression was so earnest, she couldn't say no.

"Okay." She swallowed. "Thanks."

He draped his jacket over her shoulders. It smelled like salt water and beach glass. Midnight tides and kites flying against a summer sky. Like Lucas.

She breathed deep. And as they sat shoulder-to-shoulder, watching the moon rise high over the water, as brilliant and blue as a sapphire, she thought about now nice it felt to finally let someone in.

Even for just a little while.

Later, after they'd walked home with waves lapping at their feet, they climbed the stairs of the beach house and stood between their two screen doors.

"Well, this is me." Jenna nodded toward her half of the patio.

Lucas glanced at his side. "It looks like your neighbor is a real slob."

She laughed. "Yeah, but his dog is really well-behaved, so there's that."

Their eyes met, and the air between them suddenly felt thick with meaning. It made it hard to breathe...or think...or imagine any-thing other than rising up on her tiptoes and kissing Lucas's cheek.

She took a preventative step backwards, shrugged out of his jacket and returned it to him. "Thanks for this, and for tonight. It was fun."

His eyes glittered in the moonlight. "It was."

"I guess I'll see you tomorrow."

"Yes, you will see me tomorrow." The corner of his mouth hitched into a grin. "Not that you have much of a choice."

Right. He was still her next-door neighbor. Tomorrow everything would probably go back to normal, even though a tiny part of her wished it didn't have to.

"True." She nodded. Maybe that part wasn't as tiny as she wanted it to be. "Okay..."

"Okay. Well, um. Good night." He turned to face his door.

"Good night," she said.

And then everything started to move in slow motion as he turned back around and walked a tiny step toward her. Her feet inched closer to him before she even realized what she was doing. He was going to kiss her. The warmth in his gaze and the little sparks of electricity bouncing between were a dead giveaway.

A long time ago, when Jenna had come to Tybee as a little girl, her grandfather told her about beach wishes. He said that if she wrote a wish in the sand, the tide would carry it away and someday, when the time was right, the wish would return to her, fulfilled. Thinking about kissing Lucas felt fated somehow, as if the entire summer had been leading up to this moment...as if she'd written it in the sand all those years ago.

But as their lips drew closer, Lucas's arms were suddenly around her, pulling her into a tender embrace. It was a hug, not the kiss she'd wanted so very badly.

Jenna closed her eyes. There was that smell again, like endless summer. Only this time it was paired with sweet warmth and just enough disappointment that a lump formed in her throat.

When they stepped apart, all she could do was whisper. "Okay, bye."

"Bye," he murmured. "Good night."

She turned toward her half of the duplex but glanced over her shoulder in time to see Lucas disappear behind his screen door and let out a wistful sigh that sounded as if he had a few beach wishes of his own.

Then they went their separate ways—her on one side of the fence and him on the other. But Jenna's heart lingered in the space in between.

Chapter Twelve

ALLY KNOCKED ON LUCAS'S DOOR bright and early a few days later, as had become her routine over the past few weeks. He stumbled toward the patio, yawning as usual. Was it his imagination, or did she show up earlier and earlier every time?

"Leash, please!" She grinned up at him and held out her hand.

He held up a finger and disappeared back inside for a few minutes while she waited. Once Tank was all decked out in his shell collar and Lucas had put on a fresh hoodie and pair of board shorts, he clipped the leash to the dog's collar and walked him outside to meet Ally.

"Come on, boy."

Tank practically strutted to the patio. He'd started looking forward to his morning walks with Ally. It was cute, albeit somewhat surprising, considering that Lucas still heard her peppering Tank with commands as they disappeared over the dune every morning.

Ally lit up with excitement when she saw them coming, and Lucas couldn't help but smile. Warmth filled his chest as Jenna's words from the night before came back to him.

She really likes you. They both do.

He pushed the screen door open, ignored Ally's outstretched hand and stepped out onto the deck.

"Wait." Ally glanced down at Tank and then back at Lucas. "Where are you going?"

"I thought I'd tag along today, if that's all right with you?"

She gasped and then beamed at him. "Are you kidding? Yes!"

"Here you go." Lucas handed her the leash. Tank followed the transfer with a swivel of his furry head. "Lead the way."

"Awesome." Ally skipped down the stairs with Tank bobbing faithfully alongside her.

They crossed the dune over the worn path where the sand was loose, surrounded by sea oats swaying in the gentle morning breeze. The ocean was crystal clear, bright and shimmering. At this early hour, the only other people on the beach were serious runners and fishermen looking for a morning bite.

Lucas followed Ally's lead as she turned

toward the quieter end of the island, where most of the sea turtles typically came ashore to build their nests and lay eggs. The sand farther up near the dune was marked in spots with wooden stakes and bright yellow tape, protecting the places already visited by nesting turtles. Come autumn, the beach would be crawling with tiny, fragile hatchlings making their way to the sea.

Now, all was quiet, save for the gentle swish of the waves coming ashore and Tank panting softly at the end of his leash.

"Mind telling me where we're going?" Lucas asked.

"Right here." Ally stopped near an empty wooden swing facing the water. "Sit down. It's his favorite spot."

As far as Lucas knew, Tank had never batted an eye at the swing before. But he was willing to give it a go. "Okay."

"It took him a while to warm up," Ally said.

Warm up for what? Lucas lowered himself onto the swing and nudged it into motion with his foot. "He's not really a morning dog. Or a trick dog, for that matter."

Ally smirked, then pointed at Tank and said, "Sit."

Tank obediently plopped his rear on the ground in a perfect sit position.

Lucas's mouth dropped open, and before

he could recover from the shock of what he'd just seen, Ally kept going.

"Shake." She held out her hand and placed his paw in it.

It was astounding…and one of the cutest things Lucas had ever seen.

Ally wasn't finished though, because of course not. She wasn't the kind of kid to do things halfway. If Lucas wasn't careful, she'd probably have Tank whipping up chocolate chip cookies.

"High five," she said, and Tank dutifully obeyed.

Ally stood primly, head tilted just so, as she shot Lucas a look that said, *See?*

He stared at his own dog, bewildered. "That's amazing."

"He just didn't know what he was missing." She bent and gave Tank a scratch behind his ears, then she pranced in a happy circle while the pup scampered and leapt after her.

So it was as simple as that. Tank had been set in his independent doggy ways, perfectly content on his own, until a relentless charmer moved in next door and turned his life upside down.

Why did that scenario sound so familiar?

He just didn't know what he was missing.

Maybe the kid had a point.

Jenna held the door open for Maureen as they stepped into one of the cute mom-and-pop gift shops on Tybee's Main Street.

"I told him no hot tub until he finishes the porch." Maureen made a beeline for a rack of breezy sundresses while Jenna browsed through gift items on the tables up front.

She picked up a picture frame decorated with coral and put it back down. "You think that will work?"

Maureen let out a laugh. "The man wants a hot tub."

She had a point. Ian had been talking about building a deck with a hot tub in their backyard in Savannah for months. It was only a matter of time.

Jenna considered the assortment of knickknacks until she spotted a table with a neat row of colorful ties for sale in the middle of the shop. *Aha!*

She picked up one of them—silk, the color of aqua-hued beach glass.

Maureen's eyebrow rose. "So you're buying a gift? For Lucas? From the *kids*?"

They'd already been through this. That's why Jenna had wanted to go shopping while Ally, Nick and Grayson were busy at day camp. She should have known Maureen would press for details. She'd been wearing her matchmaker expression all morning.

"The kids want to give him something for good luck since he's coming over for dinner," Jenna said as casually as possible.

She'd asked him this morning when she'd returned from dropping Nick and Ally off at summer camp and found Lucas sanding his surfboard on the deck. The invitation had popped out of her mouth before she could stop it.

"Wait. *What?*" Maureen's face lit up like a Christmas tree. "When?"

Jenna shrugged one shoulder. "Tonight."

Maybe if she acted completely nonchalant about the dinner, Maureen wouldn't make *a thing* of it.

Jenna was wrong, of course.

Maureen gasped out loud. "I can't believe we've been hanging out for over an hour and you're just telling me this now?"

"It's not a big deal." But it felt gigantic.

"Hello? You've barely dated since your divorce," Maureen oh-so-helpfully pointed out.

Which was exactly why Jenna didn't want to overthink dinner. Otherwise, she'd be a nervous wreck. The last time she'd eaten in front of Lucas, she'd mangled a crab. Who knew what would happen next?

"Yeah...well. I've been a little busy," she said.

"For the last four years?" Maureen dead-panned.

"Yes." She put the aqua tie back and considered a pink one, refusing to meet Maureen's gaze.

Jenna knew she meant well. Other than her kids, Maureen was her closest confidante. Still, the truce with Lucas was still new. Who knew if it would even last?

"It's okay to feel excited," Maureen said.

Jenna sighed. Could they not have this discussion? *Please?*

"All right, fine." Maureen held her hands up. "If it makes you feel more comfortable, it's not a big deal."

Jenna nodded. "Thank you."

"But you still need a new dress." Maureen grinned and darted back to the rack of sundresses. "What about this one?"

She held up a light blue dress with thin straps and a dramatic navy velveteen leaf design swirling over the bodice and long skirt.

It was very pretty. And very, very date-like.

"What's wrong with what I'm wearing?" Jenna glanced down at her striped shirt and cropped pants.

Maureen rolled her eyes. "You can't wear khakis on a date."

"It's not a date. It's a dinner. With the *kids*." Besides, Jenna had lived next door to

Lucas for weeks already. She was pretty certain he'd seen her in her bathrobe and fuzzy slippers on a few occasions.

"Tomato, tomahto." Maureen dangled the dress in front of her.

The shop's sales clerk appeared, seemingly out of nowhere. "Can I help you find a size?"

"No," Jenna said.

At the exact same time, Maureen smiled and blurted, "Yes."

The sales clerk glanced back and forth between them.

"Just try it on." Maureen fluttered her eyelashes at Jenna. "Please?"

She wasn't going to give in. If Jenna didn't agree to try on the dress, Maureen would probably try and wrestle her into it.

"Fine." She plucked the hanger from Maureen's grip. "But it's not a date."

"No, of course not," Maureen said, but her smile was triumphant.

And as Jenna stepped into the tiny dressing room and slid its curtain closed, she heard her best friend whispering on the other side.

"It's a date."

Chapter Thirteen

A FEW HOURS LATER, THE HOUSE was clean, dinner was ready, and Jenna was wearing the pretty blue dress.

Maureen hadn't taken no for an answer. And once Jenna had slipped it on and taken a look at herself in the mirror, she'd been easier to convince. It really was a lovely dress—slim, pretty and a little more glam than khakis without being over the top.

Still, five minutes before Lucas was due to arrive, she decided to change back into her cropped pants and trusty cardigan. Lucas would probably show up in his ordinary surfer uniform of a hoodie and board shorts. She'd invited him over for dinner with the kids. There was a zero percent chance he'd consider it a date, and here she was in a dress with spaghetti straps and her hair freshly blown out and tumbling down her back in thick waves.

What had she been thinking?

She reached to unzip the back of the dress and step out of it, but it was too late. Before her fingertips made contact with the zipper, someone knocked on the door.

It had to be Lucas.

Too late to back out now.

She took a deep breath and made her way to the living room, where she caught her first glimpse of him through the storm door on the patio. At least she thought it was Lucas—she barely recognized the handsome man standing on the deck in a crisp button-down shirt and dark, slim-cut pants. And was that a *bouquet of flowers* in his hand?

Her footsteps slowed and for a ridiculous fraction of a second, she thought she might cry. She couldn't remember the last time anyone had brought her flowers.

Her hand shook as she reached for the door knob, and when she swung the door open, they stood quietly looking at each other as if for the first time.

"Wow. You look..." She swallowed. "... different."

Lucas's gaze turned tender. Reverent. "You look incredible."

Jenna smiled. *Thank you, Maureen. I owe you one.* "Thanks. Come on in."

Lucas took a step and then stopped. "Oh." He offered her the bouquet. "These are for you."

They were wild flowers, as beautiful and free as the ocean, in a mix of vibrant colors— sunny yellow, bright violet, red and hot pink. Jenna couldn't help but think about the Rice Krispies Treats he'd loved so much.

Rainbow-colored food is my favorite type of food.

It was official. Rainbow-colored flowers were now her favorite type of flowers.

"Thank you." Joy bubbled up inside her.

Lucas stepped inside and as the sweet perfume of the wildflowers mixed with the balmy sea breeze, she smiled and inhaled deeply.

It's totally a date.

Lucas had never been on a date with children tagging along before, and he had to admit, it made things interesting. In a good way, though—especially where the salad was concerned.

He poked his fork at the pile of greenery on his plate. "So what have we got here? We've got some arugula, figs and..." He glanced at Ally. "...chocolate chips?"

"Yes, they are." She nodded and took a giant bite of romaine lettuce dotted with semisweet chocolate morsels.

"Ally insisted on making the salad," Jenna said.

"I see. It's…" *Adorable.* "Delicious."

It actually wasn't half-bad. Who needed croutons when there was chocolate? Maybe Ally was onto something.

Nick also seemed to have something up his sleeve, although Lucas couldn't quite figure out what it was. He'd spent enough time with the kid to know when something was on his mind. He finally let loose with it during the chocolate-laden salad course.

"So." Nick set down his fork and met Lucas's gaze from across the table. "We have prepared a list of questions."

Lucas nearly choked on his arugula. "For who? Me?"

"You did?" Jenna's eyes widened in what looked like genuine horror. It was kind of cute seeing her so rattled for a change.

But not quite as cute as her children grilling him to see if he was good enough for their mom. Ally had even brought a notepad. She pulled it out from beneath the dining table and flipped through its pages.

Pages…*plural.* Good grief, how many questions did they have?

Lucas suppressed a smile and prepared to face off with Nick and Ally.

"Question number one." Nick squared his slender shoulders. "Where did you grow up?"

Jenna reached for her wine glass. "Well, this is relaxing."

Lucas did his best to keep a straight face as he answered the question. "Arroyo Grande."

"Okay. My turn." Ally consulted her written list. "Who taught you how to surf?"

"The VCR." Lucas popped a bite of salad into his mouth.

Jenna laughed. With any luck, she was starting to have a good time again. He wanted this to be a nice date. Scratch that—he wanted it to be an *excellent* date, despite the impromptu interrogation.

Ally screwed up her face. "What's that?"

Really? The VCR wasn't that out of date, was it? "Proof that I'm a lot older than you."

"Okay. Next question." Nick glanced at his sister.

Ally straightened. "Oh, this one is mine. What do you like best about our mom?"

Jenna went as pink as the flowers in the bouquet he'd brought her.

"Okay, no. You don't have to answer that." She glanced around, clearly in search of a diversion. "More salad?"

Um, no. One entire bowl of leafy green vegetables mixed with candy was plenty. Nevertheless, Jenna darted to the kitchen. Behind her, he spotted crayon drawings of Tank tacked to the refrigerator.

Lucas thought for a moment, considering the question. "What do I like best?"

Nick nodded. "First thing that comes to mind."

"You *really* don't have to answer that," Jenna said as she walked back to the table. She looked almost terrified.

Didn't she realize he could name at least six things he liked about her, just off the top of his head? He even liked her nerdy little cardigans. He liked them even more than her mermaid swimsuit because they were so quintessentially *Jenna*.

But he didn't want to say anything that might be interpreted as glib. It was a meaningful question, and it deserved a meaningful answer.

He met Jenna's gaze and answered as honestly as he could. "She's full of surprises."

Jenna stopped in her tracks, salad bowl in hand. She blinked a few times, and Lucas's heart skidded to a stop when he realized her eyes were glossy with tears.

He gave her a tender smile while Nick grinned from ear to ear. Ally was so delighted by his response that she grabbed a pen from the kitchen counter and struck through the rest of her list. Lucas had passed their little test with flying colors.

He released a breath. "Can I have some more water?"

Jenna smiled. "Absolutely."

Nick and Ally exchanged a glance and collapsed into giggles.

"What are you laughing at?" Lucas dead-panned. He speared a chocolate chip with his fork. "The salad's great, by the way."

"Thank you," Ally said. Then she abandoned her notepad, and the meal proceeded without any more questions.

Lucas could breathe easy...at least for a little while.

After dinner, Jenna asked him if they could see the finished version of the video he'd prepared for the meeting with the potential summer camp investors the following day. He didn't mind, of course. He'd spent hours getting it ready, and as he'd told Jenna over crab and shrimp at Sam's, he could usually let things go once he'd done the best he could do.

But as he slid the disc into the DVD player, he had a strange feeling in the pit of his stomach. And when he sat down and waited for the video to start, he found himself watching Jenna, Ally and Nick instead of the action onscreen.

He cared about their opinions, maybe even as much as he cared what the investors had to say.

What was happening? This was supposed to be a fun evening. A date. And suddenly, it was beginning to feel like something else.

It was beginning to feel like something *more*.

He did his best to focus on the flickering images on the television screen—scenes of children running on the beach, jumping into a cool blue pool and splashing in the ocean—scenes that mirrored the time Nick and Ally had spent at Tybee all these weeks. But his gaze kept flitting back to Jenna and her kids snuggled together on the sofa, and warmth bloomed inside him, as colorful and alive as the new flowers sitting on Jenna's kitchen counter.

The video ended, and he pushed the off button on the television remote. "So. What do we think?"

Nick and Ally bounced in place on the sofa and answered him in unison. "It was awesome!"

Lucas laughed and glanced at Jenna. "How much did you pay them to say that?"

But he was pretty certain he couldn't buy that kind of enthusiasm. It felt priceless.

"You should be proud. It's really good," Jenna said.

The softness in her eyes made him wish he was sitting beside her and the kids on the couch instead of all by himself in the living room's overstuffed chair. He wasn't sure he belonged over there, though, nor did it look like there was enough room.

Who chose this furniture, anyway? Oh, right. He did. This was *his* house, both halves of it. And he still hadn't managed to bring himself to tell Jenna.

He cleared his throat. The details of the beach house rental were probably something he should get out in the open. But before he could say anything, Jenna nodded toward the kids, and Nick pulled a small square gift box out from behind one of the sofa cushions. He passed it to Ally, who in turn handed it to Jenna.

"Here." Jenna held the box toward him. "The kids got you a little something."

"What? You guys are crazy." He took the gift and ran the pad of his thumb along its carefully tied white bow.

There was no telling what was inside. Another craft project? A multi-colored dessert?

"Open it." Ally grinned at him.

Lucas untied the bow and braced himself for something covered in glitter, shells or chocolate. Maybe even all three. But when he lifted the lid of the box and peeled back a few layers of yellow tissue paper, he didn't see any of the trademark features of a homemade gift. He saw smooth burgundy fabric, dotted with tiny white polka dots. His heart felt like

Teri Wilson

it was being squeezed in a vise as he lifted a fine silk necktie from the tissue paper.

This wasn't just a gift from the kids. It was from Jenna, too.

"I don't know what to say," he said quietly. She'd cooked him dinner and invited him to spend the evening with her family. And now this...

Could it be true? After all these weeks of hiding behind her fence, had Jenna Turner finally decided to let him in?

"It's for good luck," Ally said.

Nick shrugged. "Well, you could say thank you."

Lucas laughed and unfolded the tie, trying to imagine himself wearing it.

"Now you have a tie for your meeting." Jenna tilted her head.

"You didn't have to." Lucas's throat grew thick, and he had a sudden memory of a Father's Day long ago and giving his dad a similar silk tie. "But thank you. Thank you very much."

Ally scrambled off the sofa, walked over to him and threw her arms around his neck. Lucas wasn't prepared for the sudden display of affection and sat still as stone for a moment before hugging her back.

It was too much all of a sudden—the dinner, the gift, the urge to be more to this little family than just the messy surfer next door.

He wanted to make them proud. He wanted to live up to the vision these kids seemed to have of him as someone who they should look up to...someone who *mattered*.

Lucas had no business wanting those things. He couldn't be a father figure. He didn't even know how.

You've built the life you want, remember? Simple, free, easy.

He swallowed hard. Why did *easy* suddenly seem synonymous with *empty*?

Lucas extricated himself from Ally's embrace and stood, shifting from one foot to the other. "Okay, you know what? I should probably get going."

Nick sighed. "He's not a big hugger."

They weren't going down that road. Not here. Not now.

Besides, he really did need to get back to his side of the duplex. Tomorrow was important, and he was suddenly questioning all of his priorities, which wasn't the best way to impress an investor.

"I just want to get up early and get a surf in before my meeting. You know, de-stress," he said.

Jenna rose from the sofa to stand beside him. "You're going to do great." She smiled in Nick's direction. "Well, it's a big day for everyone tomorrow. Nick has his swim trial."

Was that tomorrow? Lucas hadn't realized it was scheduled for the same day as his big meeting.

He should be there for Nick. He *wanted* to be there. But his meeting was off the island, and he wasn't sure what time he'd return.

"What's the lucky number you need to make swim team at school?" Jenna cast a quick look at Nick, but Lucas was pretty sure she knew exactly what time he had to beat. They all knew.

"1:18," Nick said.

"1:18." Jenna glanced at Lucas. "Remember?"

"Of course I remember."

Nick turned hopeful eyes on Lucas. "So you'll be there?"

He nodded. "I am going to try my hardest."

Nick's gaze shimmered with admiration. "'Cause I always do better when..."

When I'm there.

Lucas didn't let him finish. "You know what? I'll be there. I promise."

The look of relief on Nick's face hit Lucas square in the chest.

He cleared his throat. "And on that note, thank you so much for dinner. The salad was delicious. I had a really nice time."

"Me, too. Thank you," Jenna said, and Lucas realized he'd been waiting the whole summer for her to smile at him the way she was right then.

How had he not known he'd been waiting for that all along?

His breath hitched. "Good night."

"Good night," she said, and her glowing smile stayed with him while he walked back to his side of the house.

He carried it in his heart as he sat down to go over the details of his presentation one last time. Tank nestled next to him on the patio sofa and even though Lucas's laptop was open on the table, glowing in the dark beside a stack of charts and budget projections, his thoughts kept straying back to it. Time and again.

He picked up the tie and turned it over in his hands. Beside him, Tank let out a soft woof.

"I know what you're thinking." Lucas bent and kissed the top of the pup's head. "But no, this does not mean we're going to Disneyland."

Chapter Fourteen

ENNA DARTED AROUND THE KITCHEN in her favorite pajamas the next morning, slicing fruit and scrambling eggs. No pancakes today, she'd decided. No chocolate chips. This was a special day for Nick—a day that called for protein, vitamins and minerals.

She couldn't help smiling to herself as she pushed the eggs around the frying pan with a pretty turquoise spatula. Despite her mild case of nerves about Nick's swim test, she was practically giddy. Last night had been so cozy, so...unexpected. Something had definitely shifted between her and Lucas. Something important.

After Lucas had gone home, Ally and Nick kept stealing glances at her, grinning from ear to ear.

"Stop looking at me like that," she'd finally told them, but she couldn't even get the words out without a bubble of joy rising up within her.

She wasn't imagining things. Even the kids had noticed the feelings swirling around the beach house between her and Lucas. Jenna wasn't quite sure what they meant yet, but they were real.

"All right, come eat!" she called, scooping a generous dollop of eggs onto Nick's plate.

He bounded up the stairs, already dressed in his favorite swimsuit with the shark print and a striped shirt that looked an awful lot like something Lucas had worn recently.

"I want you to get all the major food groups in before your test." She added an extra spoonful of eggs to Nick's serving as he pulled out a chair.

"You need to stop worrying, Mom. I'm ready." He plopped down and picked up a fork.

"I know you are." Jenna stirred the bowl of cantaloupe and strawberries she'd prepared and slid it toward him. "I just want you to feel good. Full of energy."

He studied her as he chewed a bite of eggs. "You look happy."

The goofy grin she'd been wearing since last night hadn't gone anywhere apparently. "I'm always happy, bud."

"Yeah, but you look *extra* happy today."

"Well, I finished my draft last night. So…"
She did a happy little dance.

Finally. The book was done.

She'd been walking on air after Lucas left, too keyed up to sleep. So she'd stayed up late and finished putting the final touches on the ending. Now she could enjoy their last few days at the beach without worrying about whether or not she'd still have a career when they got back to Savannah.

"I don't think that's it," Nick said bluntly.

She focused intently on the cantaloupe. "No?"

"I think our neighbor—"

"Okay, mister." Jenna interrupted. "No time for speculation. Eat!"

She wasn't ready to discuss her feelings for Lucas with her kids. She didn't even understand them yet herself.

Nick obediently stabbed a strawberry with his fork while outside on the patio, Tank let out three happy yips.

Jenna glanced out the window on her way back to the kitchen. Her heart fluttered when she spotted Lucas heading toward his Jeep, dressed in a finely tailored suit and tie. Not just any tie, but *the* tie—the silky-smooth burgundy one she'd finally settled on at the beach shop while Maureen tried to talk her into new earrings to go with her pretty blue date dress.

He looked so handsome, so *businesslike.*
It was startling.

"I'll be back soon, buddy." Lucas waved
at Tank, then climbed into the driver's seat
and headed down the gravel drive. Off to the
meeting with his investors.

He was going to do great. Jenna just
knew it.

"Ally, breakfast!" she yelled before float-
ing to the kitchen.

It's going to be a good day.

A few hours later, Jenna's optimism took a
serious hit.

She and Ally sat on the bleachers at
summer camp, watching eight campers line
up by the pool. Two groups of boys had already gone, and now Nick and Grayson were
up, along with the other boys their age.

Jenna glanced at the empty space beside
Ally, the spot they'd saved for Lucas. She'd
expected him to turn up at least half an
hour ago when the swim trials first started,
but she hadn't heard a word from him. If he
didn't show up within the next few minutes,
he'd miss Nick's race.

He's going to be here.

Of course he was. He'd promised, and
Lucas wasn't a parent, but surely he knew
better than to make a promise to a child

that he couldn't keep. Especially a child who looked up to him as much as Nick did.

She craned her neck for a better view of the parking lot, but his Jeep was nowhere to be seen. When she swiveled her gaze back toward the action poolside, she spotted Nick sitting on the starting block of his lane. While the other boys stretched and fastened their goggles in place, he slumped with his back turned to the water and his swim goggles propped on his forehead. The dejected look in his eyes just about broke Jenna's heart.

Lucas, where are you?

Her leg jiggled. She couldn't sit still and suddenly time was moving too fast. Kayla strode to the pool's edge with a whistle around her neck and a stopwatch and clipboard in her hands.

"All right, guys. Have fun out there," she said.

Jenna had to stop herself from jumping out of her seat and asking for a time-out.

Couldn't she see that Nick wasn't ready? He'd been so confident this morning at home. So sure of himself. But that had been back when he thought he'd have Lucas there to cheer him on.

Kayla obviously sensed something was wrong, because instead of blowing her whistle and calling for the kids to take their starting positions, she approached Nick's lane with a smile.

"Nick, you're up next. Let's see if you can beat your personal best," she said.

Only his eyes moved. He didn't hop to his feet, nor did he bother adjusting his goggles. "Have you seen Lucas?"

"Um." Kayla glanced around. "I'm sure he's on his way."

Was he? Jenna was beginning to wonder.

"Line up." Kayla gave Nick's knee a gentle nudge.

He dragged himself upright on the starting block, and Jenna couldn't take it anymore.

She reached into her purse for her cell phone and dialed Lucas's number. Maybe if he was on the way, she could convince Kayla to wait.

But the phone rang and rang. It rolled over to voicemail just as Kayla's whistle pierced the air and the swimmers dove into the pool. Nick's race started with a half-hearted splash, and Jenna had no choice but to face reality.

Lucas wasn't on the way. He'd never make it by the end of Nick's race.

He wasn't even answering her call.

Lucas gazed out the window of an upscale restaurant located right on the beach, mere steps away from the surf. Frothy waves tumbled onto the shore, dotting the damp sand with shells while the two men sitting across the table from him decided the future of his summer camp.

He'd barely eaten a bite of his lunch. He hadn't realized how much he wanted this deal until now. All his talk about letting things go had actually convinced him that he wasn't personally invested in the summer camp.

But that wasn't quite true. The camp wasn't just a paycheck. It meant something to him, more now than ever before. Seeing how much the summer camp meant to Jenna's kids, especially Nick, had given him a whole new perspective the past few weeks. It wasn't just a way for Lucas to pay for a home at the beach so he could surf all the time. The camp was an important part of the community on Tybee, and if this deal went through, it could change other beach communities all over the state. Maybe even the country.

The two investors exchanged a glance and Lucas held his breath.

Finally, one of them smiled and put him out of his misery. "We'll leave the promotional piece as is and just run with it from there."

So this was happening?

There would obviously be contracts

to sign and details to hammer out, but it sounded like they'd struck a tentative deal.

Lucas nodded. "Hey, I'm open to anything as long as the integrity of the camp stays the same."

Bob, the investor Lucas had known since his Berkeley days, tossed his napkin on the table. "Well, I think we need to go out and celebrate, start talking expansion plans."

Yes!

He'd done it.

Lucas grinned, but just as he was about to agree to an impromptu celebration, his phone lit up and began vibrating on the crisp white tablecloth.

Jenna's name flashed on the tiny screen, right beneath the time display. It read 2:13. He'd been sitting at this table for more than two hours, and now Nick was probably only minutes away from his swim trial.

He had no idea the meeting had run so long, but it wasn't as if he could have gotten up and walked out. And now there was no way he'd make it back to the camp in time for Nick's race.

Still, his jaw tensed as the call rolled to voice mail.

"I'd love to," Lucas said. *I made the kid a promise.* "But I can't."

Bob frowned. "Why? Do you have a wife and kids waiting for you?"

Lucas shook his head. "You know that's not the case."

Bob was familiar with Lucas's trajectory since business school. He'd mentioned time and again how much he envied Lucas's carefree life on Tybee.

No strings. That's what Lucas was famous for, wasn't it?

"Then what?" Bob shrugged. "You've worked hard."

How could Lucas possibly explain his desire to leave? The deal still wasn't official, and as far as Bob knew, the summer camp was the most important thing in Lucas's life.

Is it, though?

"You're right. I have." Lucas nodded. Of course the summer camp was his priority. As much as he liked Jenna and her kids, they were leaving Tybee in just a few days. Nick and Ally would have school to keep them busy, Jenna would have her book and he'd have his camp. Only now it would be camps, plural. Life would go back to the way it had been before.

Whether he wanted it to or not.

Lucas cleared his throat. "Ten years in the making. I can't believe this is a go."

"Let's start planning," Bob's associate said.

The two men stood, and Lucas sat for a

moment, staring at Jenna's missed call notification on his phone.

He told himself it was already too late. Even if he left right that second, he'd never make it to Nick's race. It didn't really matter whether he was there or not. Nick had 1:18 in the bag. There wasn't a doubt in Lucas's mind the kid would make the team.

It would all work out fine. He was doing the right thing.

Then why did it feel so wrong?

Jenna could barely sit still.

All around her, people were clapping and cheering, but she didn't hear any of it. She was hyper-focused on every move Nick made. He'd had a rocky dive into the pool, but as soon as his wiry little body started moving through the water, he caught up with the other boys.

"Go Nick, go Nick, go!" she chanted.

He was almost neck and neck with Grayson in the lane beside him, which was a good sign. Grayson had been swimming on the school swim team for a year already. Nick couldn't wait until they could compete together. Swimming with his best friend was one of the biggest reasons he was so desperate to make the team.

He had to make 1:18. He just had to.

He'd be crushed if he didn't.

"Come on, come on, come on," Jenna whispered.

It was more of a prayer than a cheer as the swimmers reached the halfway mark. As soon as he reached the middle of the pool, Nick fell behind Grayson. A few strokes later, the other swimmers around him pulled ahead as well.

By the time the race was over and Nick's hand touched the pool wall, he was dead last.

Jenna was on the verge of tears as he pulled off his goggles and tossed them into the water.

Don't cry.

She couldn't let Nick think she was disappointed in his performance. She wasn't, obviously. She loved her kids unconditionally, and Nick had worked so hard on his swimming all summer long. He could never disappoint her.

But she was *definitely* disappointed in a certain adult.

Lucas should have been here. She swallowed around the lump in her throat and pasted on a smile as she clapped for Nick. *He gave Nick his word.*

Maybe she was being too hard on him... again. Lucas had been so great with Nick and Ally all summer. He'd probably gotten stuck at the investment meeting for the summer camp, which was a reasonable explanation.

Or it would have been, if he hadn't promised Nick he'd be there. Kids didn't understand excuses and explanations where promises were concerned. A promise was a promise.

One by one, the boys climbed out of the pool to dry off and accept the congratulations of their friends and family. Nick was last again, dragging himself from the water to go sit alone at one of the camp picnic tables with is towel slung around his neck.

Jenna couldn't take it.

She left Ally waiting on the bleachers so she could go give him a little pep talk. He'd tried his best, and that was all that mattered.

Grayson beat her to it, though. He walked over to the picnic table, still in his swimsuit with his goggles propped on his head, and attempted to cheer Nick up.

"Hey, Nick. There was a lot of drag in the pool." Grayson shrugged. "I felt it."

Nick offered him a weak smile. "You don't need to say that."

Grayson paused, and then gave it another go. "You want a soda?"

Nick shook his head. "I don't want anything."

Jenna took a deep breath and smiled

at Grayson as she reached them. "Nice job, Grayson."

"Thanks, Mrs. T," he said.

He was such a good kid, and a great friend to Nick. Jenna made a mental note to tell Maureen how sweet he'd been after the race.

She waved at Grayson as he headed toward the snack area. Then she joined Nick beside him on the bench. "You did good, bud. Really close. You should feel proud."

Nick's face fell. "Can you stop saying that?"

The lump in Jenna's throat grew three-fold. Her next words came out as barely more than a whisper. "I just don't want you to beat yourself up."

"Then stop talking about it, okay?" Nick stood and stomped away.

She stared after him at a loss. This was going so much worse than she'd feared. There had to be something she could say or do to fix things. But what?

Her stomach churned like it always did when she felt like she'd lost control of a situation. Seeing her kids hurt was the very worst part of parenting. She'd never get used to it. It brought out the mother bear in her like nothing else

I just need a plan. That's all.

For once, she couldn't come up with a course of action. The highest fence in the world wouldn't take away the pain in Nick's eyes.

His disappointment didn't escape Kayla's notice either. She watched him stalk toward the snack area as she took a seat beside Jenna.

"I'm sorry." She bit her lip. "I don't know what happened out there."

Jenna shook her head. "It's not your fault," she said quietly.

This was Lucas's fault, one hundred percent. Nick had been brimming with confidence until he realized Lucas had broken his promise.

She didn't want to blame him, but she couldn't help it.

"I'm surprised Lucas missed it," Kayla said, as if she could read Jenna's mind.

Jenna turned to study her expression. "Are you really?"

After all, Kayla had warned her about this very thing.

He's a sweet guy, for sure. But a family man he is not. He likes his freedom way too much.

Those had been her exact words at the summer concert. And like a fool, Jenna had forgotten all about them.

Not completely, though. Despite the flowers, despite the cozy sunset dinner at Sam's on the shore, and despite the kindness he'd shown to her kids, she'd been half expecting Lucas to be as casual about his promises as he was about leaving his porch a mess. She just couldn't help it.

On some level, she'd known this would happen. She simply hadn't wanted to believe it. When would she learn that she couldn't rely on anyone else? Had the divorce taught her nothing?

"This time, yes," Kayla said.

Her lips were pressed together, her expression solemn. Despite her words of warning, she seemed genuinely surprised Lucas hadn't materialized.

Jenna wished she could say the same.

Chapter Fifteen

T WAS AFTER DARK BY the time Lucas
finally got home, and Tank was nowhere to be found.

The doggy door on his side of the duplex
allowed Tank to dart back and forth between
the inside of the house and the deck. Normally when Lucas had been gone for longer
than a mere five minutes, his pup greeted
him on the patio with excited barks and a
wagging tail.

Luckily, before worry could fully set in,
he spotted Tank through the big bay window
on Jenna's half of the beach house. The dog
was sprawled across the sofa, spooning with
Ally, his devoted best friend. Both pup and
child were sound asleep.

As if the cozy display wasn't already
sweet enough, Jenna sat beside them, reading a book with Ally's head nestled her lap.

Lucas paused on the threshold, taking in
the homey scene. From the moment Jenna

had moved in with her ancient typewriter
and her organized storage bins, she'd made
his house a home. And now Tank looked so
much like part of the family that a dull ache
formed in his chest.

He swallowed it down and knocked on
the door.

Through the window he saw Jenna
glance in his direction and then swivel her
attention back to the hardback book in her
hands. She didn't budge from the couch,
and somewhere in the back of Lucas's mind,
alarm bells began to sound.

"I've got it," someone said.

Nick's voice. Lucas would recognize it
anywhere.

A second later, the boy came into view,
striding toward the screen door in a hoodie
and jeans. He swung the door open and
greeted Lucas with a deflated expression.

"Hey, buddy." Lucas grinned. Nick didn't
crack a smile, and that's when he knew.

He *knew* with absolute certainty.

Nick hadn't swum the time he needed to
make the team in the fall. Lucas didn't even
have to ask. It was written all over the poor
kid's face. It was also written all over Jenna's,
who'd yet to utter a peep. She stayed right
where she was, glaring down at her reading
material.

Lucas stumbled over his next words,

knowing they were wholly inadequate in the face of such profound disappointment. "Sorry I missed you earlier."

"That's fine." Nick's voice was uncharacteristically flat.

It *wasn't* fine. That much was obvious. Lucas had messed up in the worst possible way.

How could this have happened? Nick had 1:18 in the bag. He'd made the time days ago in practice and had been consistent every day since.

Only one thing about today had been different—Lucas hadn't been there, cheering him on.

He had the sudden urge to turn back time and tell Bob he couldn't go out and celebrate, but of course that wasn't possible.

He shifted from one foot to the other. "Is your mom home?"

Of course she was. She was sitting less than twenty feet away on the sofa, studiously avoiding his gaze.

Lucas didn't even know what he was saying. He was still trying to wrap his head around the fact that Nick hadn't made 1:18.

And it might have been my fault.

"Yeah." Nick gave him a weak smile. It was only the barest twitch of his lips, but Lucas would take what he could get. "I'll go get her."

Lucas nodded. He didn't dare cross the threshold and enter Jenna's half of the house. Those days were apparently over. Tank might be welcome but he most definitely wasn't.

Instead, he moved to the railing overlooking the ocean and took a deep breath of salty sea air while he waited for Jenna. The beach always had a way of calming him, and this time was no different.

Maybe things weren't as bad as he feared. It had been a long day. For everyone. Maybe he'd only been imagining her cold-shoulder treatment, and she was simply sad for Nick.

Besides, Lucas wanted Nick to make his swim team just as much as everyone else did. He hadn't intentionally done anything wrong. He'd simply attended a business meeting.

Which is exactly something my father would have said back when I was a kid.

Lucas's jaw clenched as memories flooded his consciousness—baseball games, school open houses, spelling bees. So many times when he'd searched the crowd for his dad's face. So many crushing disappointments.

Lucas had never wanted to be that kind of father, which was precisely why he'd never married, never had kids. And yet history was repeating itself all the same.

The screen door slammed, pulling Lucas back to the present as Jenna joined him on the deck.

She walked toward him, arms crossed. She was wearing another one of those cardigans he loved so much. This one was blue, the exact color of Tybee's north shore at low tide.

"I'm glad your meeting went well," she said.

He smiled. "Thank you."

"But you can't do that."

His smile dimmed somewhat. "Yes. You're right. Absolutely. I should have gotten a dog sitter. I didn't know how long it was going to take."

It was a cowardly apology. He was avoiding the real issue, and they both knew it.

"This isn't about Tank." Jenna's voice broke, splitting Tank's name into two syllables. Lucas hadn't thought he could feel worse about Nick not making the team, but he'd been wrong. "You can't make promises to kids that you can't keep."

Lucas took a ragged exhale and weighed his next words very carefully. "I thought Nick had it."

It was the truth...

And it still wasn't good enough.

Jenna shook her head. "But he didn't."

"And that's my fault?" No, it wasn't.

It couldn't be. Lucas refused to believe it because if he did, it was tantamount to admitting he'd become the one thing he'd never wanted to be. He'd become his father.

Jenna stared at him, incredulous. "It threw him."

Lucas let out a long sigh. "See, this is why I stay unattached."

"Responsibility?" She arched a brow, and he had the distinct impression she was considering adding another foot or two to the fence that still stretched from one end of the patio to the other.

"Hey, it keeps things simple."

Or it had, until he'd fallen for Jenna. Because he hadn't just fallen for her—he'd fallen for all three of them. Jenna, Nick and Ally. They were the three sweetest complications he could have ever imagined.

"So you just want to live the bachelor lifestyle forever? Never get close to anyone?" Her eyes were soft as a doe's. It made it hard for Lucas to look at her.

I can still fix this.

I have to fix this.

But he couldn't, because no matter how much he wanted to, Jenna wouldn't let him. She'd made up her mind. One mistake, and he was back on the opposite side of her fence.

"You're one to talk." He glanced at the fence and then back at her. "You literally built a barrier in your backyard because you're too afraid to let people in. Well, you cannot write people off like that."

Tears shimmered in her eyes. "This is *not* about me."

Lucas countered as gently as he could, "It kind of is."

He should know. It had taken him nearly all summer to scale that fence.

"It's about Nick," she said sharply. "He needed your support."

Lucas was treading on dangerous territory. He knew how much Jenna loved her kids. But he also knew how much trouble she had letting go. She'd admitted as much during their dinner at Sam's. She wished she could stop "trying to control things from all sides." Those had been her exact words.

Lucas took a tentative stop closer. His hands itched to hold her, but he didn't dare. "He's not a little boy anymore. He's eleven years old. He can't rely on other people to push him. He needs to learn how to push himself."

She shook her head, either unable or unwilling to hear him. Probably both. "You know what? I don't want to argue with you about this."

Of course not. She'd rather push him away.

Again.

"Fine," he said quietly.

The last thing he wanted to do was argue. He just wanted things to go back to the way they'd been before. He wanted to bring Jenna flowers. He wanted to eat arugula and chocolate chips while her kids interrogated him again.

"You can go." Jenna's gaze flitted toward his half of the beach house. Then she added half-heartedly, "...if you want."

He'd pushed her too far. He should have apologized, begged forgiveness and left it at that.

Lucas's throat grew thick. It was suddenly impossible to swallow.

I should have been there for Nick. That's what I should have done.

He searched Jenna's gaze for a glimmer of hope, any sign whatsoever that she wanted him to stay. But all he saw there was pain—pain that he'd put there himself.

So he turned around and walked to the opposite side of the fence.

Back where he belonged.

Jenna stumbled toward the kitchen the next morning and yawned while she filled the coffee pot with water. Every bone in her body ached from tossing and turning the majority of the night.

She'd hated the way she'd left things with Lucas. No matter how angry she was, she couldn't help the empty feeling that came over her every time she remembered the way he'd looked at her after she'd asked him to leave. His eyes had looked so haunted, so... desperate. If she hadn't known better, she would've thought he'd fallen in love. Not just with her, but with Nick and Ally too.

He hadn't, of course. He said so himself.

This is why I stay unattached.

Those words had hurt her more than she wanted to admit. Because no matter how very hard she'd tried to guard her heart—no matter how many walls she'd put up, both literally and figuratively—somewhere along the way, she'd fallen hard for Lucas McKinnon. She'd actually started to wonder what it might be like to be a family.

Otherwise, she would have never felt so hurt when he'd broken his promise to Nick.

Which meant on some level, this whole disaster was her fault. She'd let down her guard and look what had happened: a disaster of hurricane-like proportions.

Not anymore, she thought as she poured water into the coffee maker.

They only had two more days left at Tybee. She just had to get through the next couple of nights, and she'd never have to see Lucas's handsome face or his precious dog ever again. She and the kids could go back to Savannah and resume their normal lives.

Their normal, *safe* lives.

She pressed the start button on the coffee maker and took a deep, caffeinated inhale. "Mmm. Coffee."

While her coffee brewed, she decided to pop into Nick and Ally's room to wake them up. Maybe by the time she drank a cup—or three—of morning blend and got the pancakes going, they'd be dressed and ready to eat.

But when she pushed the door to their bedroom open, her heart leapt to her throat. Ally was sleeping soundly in her bed, but Nick's bunk was empty.

Breathe, just breathe.

He was probably just in the bathroom or something...except she'd just passed the his-and-her double bathroom the kids shared and the door had been open, the room empty. Likewise, she'd had a good view of the deck from the kitchen and it had been empty as well. The entire house was so quiet she could hear seagulls squawking down at the beach.

"Ally!" She darted to Ally's bunkbed and climbed the first few rungs of the ladder to shake her daughter awake. "Ally, honey. Where's your brother?"

Ally burrowed further beneath the covers and answered without opening her eyes. "Don't know."

Jenna's panic ratcheted up about ten notches. "He's not in his bed."

Ally lifted her head from her pillow and squinted. "He promised he'd be back."

"Be *back*?" Jenna's heart beat so hard and fast that she could hear it pounding in her ears. "From where?"

Where could Nick possibly be?

And why, oh why, did she have the sinking feeling that once she knew his whereabouts, she'd feel even less in control of things than she already did?

Chapter Sixteen

*L*UCAS WOKE TANGLED IN HIS bed sheets, feeling as if half the sand from Tybee's pristine shores had been poured into his eyes. He blinked hard and tried to figure out why he felt so terrible. Why was there such a ferocious pounding in his head?

Then he remembered.

He remembered Tank lounging on the sofa in Jenna's living room. He remembered Nick's sad expression and the look of complete and utter disappointment in Jenna's eye. He remembered feeling like he'd failed at something fundamentally important.

All he wanted to do was squeeze his eyes closed and shut everything out, but then he realized the pounding he kept hearing wasn't coming from inside his head. It was real— and coming from the patio.

Someone was banging on his door, and

that someone sounded a lot like Jenna. "Lu-cas!"

The knocking was constant, her voice piercing. But beneath the fog of sleep, Lucas heard a desperation in her tone that made him drag himself out of bed. She yelled his name three more times in the seconds it took for him to pull on a pair of jeans and make his way to the door.

"All right. All right," he said. "It's too early for drama."

He'd hoped after a good night's sleep, she would decide to accept his apology and they could end the summer on a good note. Clearly that wasn't the case.

But he took one look at Jenna and knew she wasn't there to rehash the events of yesterday.

She stood on the patio, pounding on his door with a glimmer of wild panic in her eyes. Then she said the words that made the floor feel like it was about to fall away beneath his feet.

"What is Doran's Cove?"

He blinked. Doran's Cove was the secret spot by the Cockspur Island lighthouse—the place where he'd taken Nick the day they'd gone for a bike ride instead of swimming laps at the pool. Even more significantly, it was the spot where Lucas had forced himself to swim through a riptide current to the lighthouse and back when he'd been Nick's age. He'd done something monumentally stupid in order to prove himself when he'd felt like he couldn't swim fast and hard enough... when he'd been let down and afraid.

Just like Nick had been last night.

No.

Lucas had told Nick that story so he would understand that he hadn't always been the surfer and strong swimmer he was today. Lucas had simply been trying to identify with him and give the boy some inspiration. He certainly hadn't meant for Nick to follow in his ill-chosen footsteps.

The next few seconds passed as a blur as Lucas sprang into action. He helped buckle Jenna and Ally into the Jeep, then ran to the driver's side and guided the car onto Tybee's Main Street in a cloud of dust and gravel. As they sped down the road that ran parallel to the bike path and the island's historic trail, he tried to figure out how he was going to explain to Jenna why Nick would sneak out for an early morning swim in choppy waters. All she knew was that he'd told Ally he was headed to Doran's Cove and he'd be back before breakfast.

Lucas wished he could convince himself that he was wrong and that Nick had just gone there to ride his bike. But that didn't make sense. In his heart, he knew exactly what Nick was doing down there. Jenna, on the other hand, had no idea.

"I don't understand why Nick would do this. He's never snuck out before." She stared hard out the window, as if she thought she might be able to see all the way to Doran's Cove if she tried hard enough.

"I'm sure he had his reasons," Lucas said quietly.

He had to tell her the truth. All of it. But he wasn't sure how, because there were other things he had to say too. Important things—things that would lead to goodbyes.

"How did he even know about this place?" She shook her head.

Lucas couldn't put it off any longer. He turned to look at her and then refocused on the road, swallowing around the dry lump in his throat.

In the rearview mirror, he could see Ally glancing back and forth between them. Her eyes swam with unshed tears.

Jenna went still. "What?"

Somehow, Lucas forced the words out. "I brought him here."

"You *what*?" Jenna gaped at him as if he were a stranger. As if they'd never played volleyball together on the beach or shared cracked crab beneath a sweeping beach sunset.

I'm still me, he wanted to say. *We're still us.*

He inhaled a ragged breath. The cove was less than a quarter mile away. "This spot was really important to me when I was a kid. I thought maybe it would help."

"How could this possibly help?" Her tone was incredulous.

Message received: Lucas didn't know the first thing about kids or what they might need.

"I just wanted to give him some encouragement." He gripped the steering wheel so tight that his knuckles went white.

"I can't believe you." Jenna shook her head. "I can't believe that you would do this."

What was he supposed to say?

You're right. I made a mistake. I wanted to be there for Nick, but I didn't know how. I'm not his dad, but I care about him.

I care about all of you.

Now wasn't the time. The last thing Jenna wanted to hear right now was that he thought he might be falling in love with her. Time was running out, though. Would he ever have the opportunity to tell her how he felt? Not only were Jenna and the kids going to be on their way back to Savannah, tomorrow he'd be leaving as well. But she wouldn't want to hear about that right now either. All she could think about was Nick, and Lucas couldn't blame her.

So instead, he said the only thing that mattered.

"I'm sorry."

Jenna couldn't look at Lucas anymore. It was too confusing. She was so angry with him, but at the same time, she wanted to cling to him. She wanted him to wrap his arms around her and hold her like he'd done after their dinner on the pier.

She was tired of trying to keep everything under control. So very tired. Just once she wished she could lean on someone for help. Not just anyone, though.

Him.

Lucas.

It didn't make any sense. He should have been the absolute last person in the world she'd want to turn to for comfort.

She was being irrational, that was all. Her heart was simply having a difficult time catching up with her head. Because she knew falling for Lucas had been a mistake. *Clearly.*

Why was it so hard to remember that fact, even when she was half out of her mind with worry about Nick?

She bit down hard on her bottom lip to

keep it from trembling. She refused to cry in front of Ally. Jenna's daughter was sitting in the very middle of the backseat, eyes wide and searching.

Everything will be fine, she wanted to tell her. But every time she tried to say the words, they stuck in her throat.

Time was going by so slowly. Minutes had passed since she'd first spotted Nick's empty bunk bed, but they felt like hours. After what felt like a century, Lucas steered the Jeep to the end of a sandy clearing marked by palm trees and southern red cedars swaying in the breezy sea air.

Jenna barely waited for the car to stop. The moment it came to a halt, she unfastened her seatbelt and jumped out. A shiver coursed through her, and she pulled her cardigan tighter around her torso realizing she was still wearing the pajamas she'd slept in the night before. There hadn't been time to change.

Nick is okay.

We'll find him, and he's going to be just fine.

She blinked against the wind and ran a few steps. Lucas materialized beside her, and she wasn't sure how. She hadn't even registered the fact that he'd exited the driver's side of the car.

"I see his bike." She pointed at it, leaning

against a tree with Nick's familiar blue helmet dangling from the handlebars. A similar pink, child-sized bike was parked beside it.

At least he wasn't here alone, although at this point, Jenna wasn't sure whether that was good or bad news.

"Then he's got to be down there," Lucas said.

And despite all the very conflicting feelings she had about him at the moment, his presence beside her filled her with relief.

Behind Lucas, Jenna spotted Ally climbing out of the Jeep.

"Stay here, sweetie," Jenna said.

She could only worry about one child at a time right now. She needed to know Ally was somewhere where she couldn't get hurt or wander into the water while they were searching for Nick.

"Okay," Ally called. The poor thing sounded terrified.

When all of this was over, Jenna would make things up to her somehow. Chocolate. Pancakes. A movie day snuggled under soft blankets. Just the three of them.

She'd been such a fool to think they needed someone else, least of all Lucas. If only he'd stayed on his side of the fence, they wouldn't be here right now.

At the thought of her little protective barrier, Lucas's words from the night before came drifting back to her, like a kite on the wind.

You literally built a barrier in your backyard because you're too afraid to let people in. Well, you cannot write people off like that.

She shook her head, as if she could forcibly rattle them from her memory while she and Lucas raced toward the surf. In the distance, she could see three small figures in the water, making their way to the beach from the lighthouse just offshore.

"He'll be okay. He's a strong swimmer," Lucas said, running beside her.

Just the sound of his voice took the edge off of her panic. As she and Lucas drew closer, the three swimmers stood upright in the shallows and waded onto the beach. Foamy waves crashed around their ankles, and Jenna recognized her son's slender frame at once.

Thank God.

Thank God, thank God, thank God.

"Nick! *Nick!*" She ran faster, her flip-flops filling with sand.

She was close enough to hear his conversation with the kids on either side of him now—a boy and girl she recognized from summer camp.

"That was not as easy as it looked," one of them said.

The little girl pushed wet hair from her

face. "I think I drank like half the ocean. And maybe a fish."

"Who cares, we did it!" Nick grinned. Then he looked up and his gaze collided with hers. "Oh no."

"Who's that?" The other boy paused.

"That's my mom." Nick stood still while his mother closed the distance between them and threw her arms around him.

He was soaked, covered in sand and goosebumps. Jenna didn't care—she needed to touch him and inspect every inch of his wet little body to make sure he wasn't hurt.

"Nick! Honey, are you okay?" She pulled back so she could search him for any signs of injury.

"Yeah." He nodded as she ran her hands over his head.

Finally convinced her son was still in one piece, Jenna cupped his face and locked her gaze with his. "What were you thinking?"

"I thought I'd get home before you noticed." The crisp morning breeze made him shiver, but his voice was even. Determined.

Jenna planted her hands on his shoulders, wishing she could somehow keep him there—just an arm's length away. Always. "Do you have any idea how many things are wrong with that statement?"

He looked past her, toward Lucas, standing alone by the dunes.

Then he shook his head. "You don't get it."

He was right. She didn't get it, nor did she want to. She just wanted her son to promise he'd never try anything this crazy and foolish again.

Why wasn't he saying that to her? Didn't he know what she needed to hear right then?

"You're right. I don't. Do you have any idea how dangerous that was?" Her voice trembled with an unsettling combination of anger, confusion and relief. Likewise, her hand shook as she pointed toward the cluster of palm trees at the top of the dune. "I want you to go stand up there next to your bike with your sister and wait for me. We're going to talk about this on the walk home."

They couldn't ride back to the house with Lucas. It would be too awkward, plus she'd need the walk to clear her head and talk to Nick without an audience.

Nick took a few steps until he was positioned halfway between Jenna and Lucas. Stuck in the middle. "Why can't we go back with Lucas?"

Jenna fully expected Lucas to echo Nick's suggestion and offer to drive them back home, but instead he shook his head. "Sorry, bud. I've got a few things I need to take care of."

His voice was flat, his arms were crossed,

and Jenna started feeling inexplicably pan-
icked again.

Nick frowned. "Like what?"

Lucas's gaze shifted to Jenna's as he answered Nick's question. "I'm actually leaving
tomorrow."

What?

Jenna's heart thudded.

She and the kids still had two more days
at Tybee. Where was he going? Lucas hadn't
said a word about leaving. Then again, she
hadn't given him a chance to say much of
anything the night before. Or this morning.
She'd been doing most of the talking for the
past twenty-four hours.

And the more she said, the bigger the
mess she made.

Lucas took a deep breath. "I'm going to
go scout some locations for camps."

Jenna wrapped her arms around herself.
She felt instantly distraught upon hearing
this surprise news, and then furious. Not
with Lucas—with herself.

"Go on," she said to Nick, motioning toward his bicycle. "I'll meet you up there in a
minute."

This time Nick listened and jogged
toward the palm trees without argument,
leaving a trail of footprints behind him in the
sand. Jenna's gaze lingered on them for a
moment, and then she turned to face Lucas.

"Look, this is my fault." She didn't want to blame him or argue. She just wanted to go back to the person she'd been at the beginning of the summer. "I should've trusted my gut."

Lucas's expression crumpled. "What's that supposed to mean?"

It meant she'd been right all along. Lucas was totally Mr. Slack. He'd *been* Mr. Slack this entire time and she'd been too busy falling for him to notice.

How could she have been so foolish?

Yes, he was charming. And yes, much to her astonishment, he'd even been kind of great with her kids. But that didn't make him a good influence. He knew nothing about being a good role model. Nick had never even thought about sneaking out, much less swimming to the lighthouse and back before she'd welcomed Lucas into their lives.

"Nothing. It doesn't matter anymore." She shook her head and realized her teeth had started chattering.

"It clearly does. I mean, look at you." He stepped closer and ran his hands up and down her arms in a gentle, soothing motion. It felt so good, so comforting that she almost wept.

No.

She took a backward step. Letting him

get close was how she'd ended up in this situation.

"I'm *fine*." She lifted her chin. "Remember?"

Lucas grew still. Quiet. So quiet she could hear a crab skitter past them on the sand and then nothing but the gentle push and pull of the tide. It rose and fell in tender harmony with the moon—a natural dance as old as time.

Jenna had never felt such kinship with the sea before. She knew now what it was like to be swayed by a lovely, irresistible force of nature. Lucas was sand and salt, sea and sky. The beach was in his veins. He belonged here.

But she didn't. The summer was ending, and the time had come to stand her ground. After all, Lucas himself had said it best.

"You were right." She looked straight into his rich brown eyes one last time before she walked away. "Furry kids are the only kind you should handle."

Chapter Seventeen

A FEW HOURS LATER, AFTER SHE'D showered and washed off the lingering bits of sand and maternal anguish, Jenna sat at the kitchen counter icing cupcakes with Ally.

Chocolate ones, obviously.

"Do you really think they'll like them?" Ally asked as Jenna swirled a generous dollop of frosting on one of the tiny cakes.

"Double fudge cupcakes for the last day of camp? Who wouldn't?" She'd whipped them up from a boxed mix as soon as they'd returned from Doran's Cove, desperate to make the beach house feel like home again. Cozy. *Safe*.

Now the smell of chocolate lingered in the air, but Jenna still felt strange and unmoored. Why she felt that way was no big mystery.

While she'd been elbow-deep in cupcake batter, Nick had showered and then gone straight to his room and shut the door. He still hadn't emerged. Jenna had pressed her ear to the door a few times to assure herself that he hadn't tried to sneak out again, but even his presence hadn't made her feel any better.

She didn't have this kind of relationship with her kids. They talked about things and trusted each other with their feelings. But Nick had been sullen and quiet on the walk back from Doran's Cove. Sooner or later, she was going to have to hash things out with her son. The longer they went without speaking, the worse she felt.

Maybe that's why she seemed to be icing the same cupcake over and over again. It was piled high with a towering mound of frosting. Perhaps she should step away from the chocolate before somebody got hurt.

Jenna placed the cupcake on the platter alongside the others and set down her frosting spatula. She smiled at Ally. "You finish the sprinkles. I'm going to go talk to your brother. All right?"

Ally grinned and plunged her hand into a bowl brimming with rainbow-colored sprinkles. She tossed a handful of them onto the cupcakes as Jenna left the room.

When she reached the kids' bedroom, she knocked once or twice before pushing the door open. "Hey."

Nick was situated on the bottom bunk with his backpack beside him, reading a book. He'd finally decided to get started on his summer reading, apparently.

"Can we talk?" she said, lingering in the doorway.

He closed the book and set it aside. "Sure."

Jenna crossed to the other side of the room and took a seat on the adjoining bottom bunk. Their knees were only inches apart. She felt better already, having him close.

Keeping her voice as even and calm as possible, she said, "So you want to tell me what happened this morning?"

Nick shrugged. "I told you. I just wanted to surprise you."

"By sneaking out?" Just saying it made her stomach churn. "That's not a good surprise."

"I didn't mean to scare you." He blinked wide, earnest eyes. Sunlight streamed through the bedroom window, illuminating the dusting of freckles across his nose and cheeks.

Sometimes—times like now—the fierceness of the love Jenna had for her kids snuck up on her and took her breath away. Being a parent was the toughest job in the world, but worth all the heartache a million times over.

"I know, but you did," she said.

"I know. I'm sorry." He sighed. "It's just

I wanted to do it and then tell you, so you wouldn't have to worry."

Jenna felt herself smiling. "Honey, that's the beauty of being a mom. I'm always going to worry about you. Both of you, for the rest of my life. I'm just trying to understand why you did it."

"I just had to prove I could."

"To who?" She did her best to keep any bitterness from her tone. "Lucas?"

"*Myself.*" There was an unwavering firmness in his voice. He paused, then his words were laced with soft sincerity. "I don't want to be afraid of failure anymore."

Jenna took a moment to consider his explanation. She thought about how nervous he'd been at the swim trials when he realized Lucas wouldn't be there to push him to swim his fastest. And then she thought about how afraid of her own writing she'd been for most of the summer, how she'd second-guessed every sentence she typed.

It wasn't a way to live. She knew that as well as anyone did, but she wasn't sure she could change. With Lucas, she'd just about been ready to try. And then circumstances intervened, and she crawled back into her safe little shell, just like the hermit crabs that lived in the tide pools down at the shore.

As safe as it felt to retreat behind her barrier, she wasn't sure she wanted to pass that kind of attitude on to her children. She wanted them to be brave and strong.

"I get it. I really do." She nodded. "How do you feel now?"

"Like I did my best, like maybe that's enough." Nick's gaze shifted to his lap. "Sounds stupid, right?"

"No," Jenna said, pausing to wait until he met her gaze again. "But it does sound a lot like someone we know."

She arched an eyebrow.

"It wasn't his fault, Mom. Lucas didn't tell me to do it." Nick blew out a breath.

Jenna stood and lingered once again in the doorway. They'd said what they needed to say. Hopefully, Nick would talk to her next time he wanted to prove something to himself and she'd do her best to understand.

But as far as Lucas was concerned, she wasn't budging.

"I'm sorry, bud. But I don't want to talk about our neighbor anymore, okay?" She leaned against the doorframe and did her best to ignore the rebellious flutter in her belly at the thought of him.

"But he leaves tomorrow," Nick implored.

As if she could forget. She'd been glancing at the clock all day, wondering what he was doing on the other side of the fence. Folding his clothes and putting them his suitcase? Packing food, treats and toys for Tank?

She smiled to herself at the thought of them together, and then she remembered the terrible thing she'd said to him on the beach earlier this morning.

A weight settled on her heart. Maybe that was just the price of being safe.

"Then I guess we only have one more day to get through," she said. Nick didn't look convinced. Maybe a little chocolate with rainbow sprinkles would do the trick. "Come on, let's get a cupcake before your sister eats them all."

It was worth a try.

The next morning, Jenna slipped into yoga pants and a tank top for her last walk on the beach with Maureen. But before she dropped off Nick and Ally for their final day at summer camp, she whipped up one last batch of homemade beach pancakes.

Unfortunately, Ally was going to have to make do with the plain old-fashioned buttermilk variety, because there wasn't a morsel of chocolate left in the pantry. Summertime was truly coming to an end.

Jenna poured a ladle of batter into the pan she'd used nearly every morning for the past five weeks and looked around the now-familiar kitchen. Its beach glass hues were still so soothing. Next year, they'd have to stay at a different house. She couldn't take going back to being just Lucas's neighbor again.

She'd miss this place, she realized. Even

after all that had happened, all the mistakes she'd made and all the tiny pieces of her heart she felt like she was leaving behind. Scattered like seashells.

She took a deep breath and turned to face her laptop, sitting open on the kitchen counter opposite the stove. Her draft email that she'd written to her publisher, Stan, was ready and waiting to be sent. The first draft of her manuscript was already attached. All she had to do was click the send button.

Her cursor lingered, and the same frustrating doubts swirled in her mind. What if the story wasn't as good as her first novel? What if Stan hated it? Would the publishing company give her another chance, or would they cancel her contract and call it a day?

Maybe she should read through the manuscript one more time.

But then she sighed and closed her eyes and thought about her conversation with Nick yesterday.

I don't want to be afraid of failure anymore.

Neither did Jenna. Nor did she want the harrowing experience at Doran's Cove to be forgotten. It had to count for something, didn't it?

If her eleven-year-old son could figure out how to be happy with his best efforts, despite the results, couldn't she? Shouldn't she at least try and let go, just this once?

She opened her eyes, moved the cursor over the send button and clicked.

There. It was done. She'd come to the beach with a goal to finish her book and meet her deadline, and she'd made it happen. She should be thrilled.

For reasons she didn't want to contemplate, she felt only a nagging sense of emptiness. So she closed the laptop and turned back to her pancakes before they burned.

She flipped each one over with a turn of her spatula as Ally and Nick thundered up the stairs and dropped into stools at the kitchen counter behind her.

"Hey, Mom. Can we go outside and play for a bit?" Nick said.

"You need to get ready for camp." Jenna stared absently at the bubbles rising to the surface in the batter.

"But we already are." Ally chuckled.

Jenna turned around, and sure enough, both of her kids were dressed and ready to go. Nick's t-shirt matched his shorts, and Ally had even remembered to brush her hair. It was the first morning of the entire summer that Jenna hadn't needed to micromanage their morning routines.

This is new.

And she had to admit, it was also kind of wonderful.

"I'm proud of you both for getting yourselves ready." She forced her lips into the widest smile she could. "But no. Not today."

If she let them play outside and Lucas was out there, she'd probably be forced to find them and drag them to the table when breakfast was ready. And she just couldn't face him.

Or maybe she couldn't face saying goodbye. After all, he was leaving today. Either way, she was keeping her kids and her heart on the proper side of the fence.

"Your pancakes are almost ready," she said.

Then she turned back to the stove so she wouldn't have to see Nick and Ally's defeated expressions.

Lucas ran his sander over the surfboard he'd been refurbishing all summer, pausing once or twice to glance over the fence toward Jenna's patio.

Okay, so maybe it was more than once and twice. Maybe it was closer to ten or twenty times.

He wasn't in any hurry to finish his board. In fact, he didn't need to be working on it at all since he was about to go on a road trip for several weeks. There were definitely other matters that needed his attention.

But he'd been hoping to get a chance to see Ally and Nick one last time before he left. Maybe if he was really, really lucky, he'd get to see their mom too.

He didn't get it. The kids were usually out and about this time of day, playing on the deck or searching for new turtle nests on the dunes. The time had come and gone for Ally to take Tank for his early morning walk.

Lucas powered down the sander and glanced at his scruffy sidekick, lying on the porch swing with his chin resting on his paws. The beautiful disaster of a shell collar Ally had made for him was holding up surprisingly well. Not a single scalloped seashell had fallen off.

But Lucas wasn't focusing much on the collar. He couldn't see much past the melancholy softness in Tank's brown eyes. "It's a little quiet, buddy. You want to talk to me?"

Tank lifted his head a fraction of an inch, grunted and then resumed his pouting position.

"What are you thinking?" Lucas said.

He stole another glance over the fence. He knew exactly what the poor dog was thinking. Tank was wondering if the beach house had always been this quiet before Jenna and the kids moved in. After weeks of

Ally's constant chatter and swimming questions from Nick, the silence was unsettling.

Lucas didn't like it, and judging by his dog's drooping ears and sad little puppy-dog eyes, neither did Tank.

Lucas unplugged the sander and gave up on getting any work done on the board. He couldn't concentrate. He'd botched things up really thoroughly, hadn't he? He'd managed to break his dog's heart as well as his own. Possibly Jenna's.

Maybe it was a good thing he didn't have any houseplants. He probably would have broken their little leafy hearts, too.

"It's going to be all right," he promised, willing himself to believe it. Tank's nose twitched, then he opened his mouth to let out a squeaky dog yawn. The pup always yawned when he was sad.

Lucas offered his best friend a reassuring smile. "A change of scenery will do us both good."

The beach was windy—breezier than Jenna had seen it in the entire time they'd been at Tybee. It seemed appropriate though, since change was blowing in from all sides.

That was the thing about the shore though, wasn't it? The tide was its only constant. It washed in and out, over and over again, stirring up sand, moving things around. Shells, driftwood, tiny silver fish... even the shore itself. Next year, everything would look the same but different.

Kind of like the way Jenna felt while she stood alongside Maureen and watched Kayla address the kids on their final morning at camp.

This summer had changed Jenna. She might look the same on the outside, but on the inside, she felt like she'd been tossed overboard during a stormy sea. It was beginning to wear on her in a major way.

She crossed her arms and focused on Kayla, standing in the middle of the crowd of children, wearing a red long-sleeved t-shirt, jean shorts and her ubiquitous whistle around her neck.

"We've got absolutely no agenda today." Kayla grinned, and the wind whipped her blonde hair around her face. "I just want you to go get out there and play hard."

The kids exchanged happy glances, excited to make the most of their last day at the beach. Only Ally stuck her hand in the air, classroom style.

Kayla pointed at her. "Yes, Ally?"

"Since it's the last day, can we get half off M&M's?" Ally shot her a hopeful grin.

Jenna wanted to remind her about the double fudge cupcakes they'd brought. She and Ally had made so many of them the night before that each camper could probably eat two and they'd still have cupcakes leftover. But before she could say anything, Kayla laughed and promised Ally a discount on M&M's.

Then she blew her whistle and the kids sprinted toward the ocean, yelling and cheering into the wind.

Jenna and Maureen began their beach walk with much less enthusiasm, at least on Jenna's part.

Maureen chatted away beside her, tossing out suggestions for tomorrow's trip back to Savannah. "We could always caravan or get lunch or talk."

Jenna trudged on.

And on.

She didn't realize she was walking too fast for Maureen again until her friend quit moving altogether.

"All right, stop. You need to vent, or talk plans, or do something normal. Because you're freaking me out with all this silence."

"I'm sorry." Jenna winced.

"Don't be sorry. Just..." Maureen threw up her hands. "Talk to me!"

Jenna wanted to, but she didn't know where to start. Everything was such a mess. "I don't know what to say."

Maureen wasn't going to let her off the

hook that easy. Because of course not. "It's okay to feel disappointed. I liked him too."

She shook her head. "This isn't about Lucas."

"No?" Maureen frowned. "Then what is this about?"

Okay, it was *totally* about Lucas.

But Jenna didn't have to admit it because Maureen already knew. That's what best friends did—they read one another's minds when the occasion really warranted it. And if any occasion ever did, it was this one.

"Maybe you should just talk to him." She shrugged. "It might make you feel better."

Or it might make her feel even worse. Which was probably the more likely scenario given how her last two encounters with Lucas had gone.

She'd said such terrible things. She'd lashed out because she'd been afraid—not just for Nick, but for herself. The truth of the matter was that she just wasn't ready to fall in love.

Too late.

She shook her head. "I think we've already said way too much."

Besides, Lucas was probably already gone on his road trip. Even if he wasn't and by some miracle, they made up, Jenna and the kids already had one foot out the door.

The rental on the beach house ran out in less than twenty-four hours.

"We're leaving tomorrow. It's better this way." She nodded in an effort to make herself believe what she was saying.

"It's certainly safer," Maureen countered.

She said it like it was a bad thing—like Jenna wasn't just trying to protect herself and her kids, but as if she was hiding instead.

Maybe because you are.

She took a deep breath. She didn't want to stop and examine her life right now. If she did, she was afraid she might be disappointed with what she'd find.

"Do you mind if we pick up the pace a little? I just want to keep moving," she said.

Maureen nodded. "Sure."

Jenna took off walking again, the sand swallowing her footsteps, but no matter how fast or long her strides, the beach stretched out before her, bathed in beautiful silvery light.

Chapter Eighteen

JENNA TRIED TO CRAM A stack of books into the last of her organizational bins after they got home from summer camp, but it was no use. She had zero room left to pack anything. Too bad Tybee Island didn't have a Container Store. Or perhaps a moving van.

Also, weren't they leaving with approximately ten pounds less chocolate than when they'd arrived? Jenna assumed they'd have plenty of space.

This is ridiculous. She shook her head as she turned the books sideways and tried to slide them into the side of the bin. Still no luck.

"The car is already filled to the brim. I don't understand where all this stuff came from." Did she really need her gigantic hardback thesaurus? Could she leave it behind and start using an app instead? Nope. She was way too old-school for that. She'd no sooner part with her antique typewriter.

Ugh, the typewriter! She hadn't packed that yet either, and they were scheduled to leave bright and early the following morning.

"I swear we didn't bring this much," she muttered.

Nick strolled into the room and tucked a pair of earbuds into his backpack, already packed and sitting in one of the living room chairs.

"Well, I'm almost done with my stuff." He pulled a face. "Ally, not so much."

Jenna looked up from the books in her hand, pausing when she caught sight of Nick standing with his back to the big picture window and its dazzling ocean view.

The water sparkled like diamonds in the late afternoon sun. A group of pelicans flew in a perfectly arranged V against the sweeping blue sky. No matter how many times she visited the island, its beautiful beaches never failed to take Jenna's breath away.

But it wasn't the sea view that made her throat clog with emotion all of a sudden. It was her son—Nick, her sweet little boy. Except he didn't seem so little anymore. He was a little taller than he'd been when they'd first moved into the beach house. His favorite blue t-shirt wasn't quite as baggy as it had once been, and he was definitely going to need a few new pairs of longer shorts when they got back home to Savannah.

But the changes that caught her so off guard weren't strictly physical. Nick had a new air about him now. He seemed to have become more self-assured overnight, more confident. He even carried himself differently.

So much had happened since they'd come here, and somewhere along the way, her shy little boy had become a young man.

"What did I do now?" He froze and shot her a questioning glance.

She was staring.

"Nothing." Jenna smiled at her boy, but her lips trembled and before she knew what was happening, she realized she was blinking back tears.

Her smile turned watery. "You just look so grown up—even from these last five weeks."

Had it really been only five weeks? It felt like a lifetime...on *so* many levels.

Nick eyed her as she crossed the room to stand beside him in front of the window. "Are you seriously crying right now?"

"What? Nooo. I just have overactive tear ducts." She dabbed at the corners of her eyes in a wholly ineffectual effort to keep the tears at bay.

It was beginning to be a problem. She'd been crying off and on all day, blinking back tears during her walk with Maureen and now this.

I'm kind of a mess.

Saying goodbye to this place had never been so hard.

"Riiight," Nick said.

She sniffed. So much for trying to seem stoic. "But you do look grown up, though."

A glimmer of pride shone in those hazel eyes she knew so well. "I kinda learned a lot this summer."

"Yeah. Like what?" Jenna settled herself onto the arm of an easy chair, and Nick did the same opposite her.

"Like chocolate doesn't go with everything," he said with a grin.

"Very true." She nodded and tried her best not to think about Lucas choking down his arugula-chocolate chip salad like a trooper. His enthusiasm had been downright heroic.

"Bunk beds are super uncomfortable," Nick added. Lesson learned.

Jenna laughed. "I totally agree."

"And..." Nick's voice drifted off as his attention snagged on something he saw out the window.

Jenna followed his gaze and spotted Lucas in the gravel driveway, loading boxes into the back of a large black SUV. She blinked hard and looked away. "And?"

"And..." Nick turned to face her again, and his smile seemed lit from within. "You miss one hundred percent of the shots you never take."

His words made Jenna feel numb all over. It sounded like something Maureen might have said all those times she'd tried to convince her to take a chance on dating.

On Lucas.

On *life*.

Instinct told her to change the subject and stick to something less painful, something safe. But how long was she going to keep trying to guard her heart? Even when she kept herself tucked safely behind walls, she *still* managed to get her heart broken.

She'd been doing her level best to get through the remaining few hours until Lucas was gone and she could leave this summer behind for good. She knew she should tell him goodbye—she owed him that much—but she couldn't seem to do it. And deep, deep down, she knew it wasn't what she wanted. Not now, and maybe not ever.

So maybe playing it safe really wasn't the answer. Maybe living her life meant joining the game instead of watching from the sidelines, hoping not to get caught up in the fray.

Maybe rather than protecting herself and her kids, all this time she'd simply been too afraid to take the shot.

"Who told you that?" she said softly.

Nick's eyes danced. "Lucas."

Of course it had been him. He'd done his best to be a friend to Nick. A role model. He'd also tried to give her the same exact advice, and she'd thrown the precious act of kindness back in his face.

I've been so wrong.

But perhaps it wasn't too late to make things right.

"See?" Her chest felt light all of a sudden, flush with hope. "This was a *very* grown-up conversation."

She smiled and nodded toward the bedroom he shared with Ally and the two loathsome bunk beds. "Now go finish packing."

He hopped off the chair as Jenna stood to sneak a glance at Lucas out on the driveway, still loading things into the car. The sight of him filled her like warm sunshine.

"Nick?" she said.

He walked back toward her carrying a Mason jar filled with the seashells he'd found on his morning beachcombing adventures with his sister.

Jenna took a deep breath. "I think I need to go talk to him."

"You do?"

Butterflies beat nervous wings against her insides as she stepped away from the window. "Yeah. I think so."

"Then go." Nick smiled his new grown-up smile and pointed toward the door. "Like now!"

She quickened her pace. By the time she reached the patio, she'd broken into a full-on run with her flip-flops smacking the wooden planks of the deck beneath her feet.

She didn't allow herself to think about whether or not he'd want to talk to her again after their terrible conversation at Doran's Cove. She'd simply have to convince him to hear her out—she'd beg if she had to.

But what if she was too late? What if he'd already gone?

Impossible. He'd been standing beside the SUV only moments ago. He couldn't have left so quickly.

But as Jenna made her way down the patio stairs, the sound of an engine roaring to life made her heart stop. And when she reached the gravel drive, the big vehicle rolled away, along with every bit of her newfound hope.

"Lucas, wait! Lucas, stop. Stop. Lucas! Wait!" She chased after the SUV, but it kept moving toward the street until she was left standing in front of the beach house alone.

"Oh come on! No." She slowed to a stop, breathing hard. "I was like two feet away."

The car kept going, and all Jenna could do was stare at its disappearing bulk and wonder how she was going to explain to her kids that she'd really and truly let Lucas leave without any of them telling him good-bye.

But then a voice called out from the upper deck of the duplex, and it belonged to the one person in the world she most wanted to see. "Are you talking to yourself down there?"

She whipped her head around and sure enough, Lucas was leaning against the railing, watching her from above. To her immense relief, he even looked a little bit happy to see her.

He cocked his head, and a smile lingered on his lips. "Because if you are, we might need to find you some more friends."

Hope rekindled, and Jenna's heart swelled with joy. She grinned up at him, breathless. There was so much to say, and she wasn't sure where to start. Lucas was wrong, though—she didn't need to find any new friends.

She only needed him.

Lucas hadn't seen Jenna smile for two long days, but catching his first glimpse of the dazzling grin on her upturned face the moment she realized he hadn't gone anywhere had definitely been worth the wait.

"You're still here?" she said, and then

she nibbled on her lip while her cheeks flushed pink.

He loved it when she blushed. Smart, capable Jenna Turner could try and control things all she wanted, but the blossoming color on her peaches-and-cream complexion told him that some things couldn't be contained.

"Yep. There was a last-minute change of plans." He pushed away from the railing, walked down a few steps and then paused.

"Good. I mean..." She blew a lock of hair from her face, shoved her hands into the pockets of her jean shorts and then promptly removed them. "Hi."

Lucas couldn't help but smile. He'd never imagined he'd *ever* see Jenna at a loss for words. It was sweet, and more than a little bit adorable.

"This is good because..." She took a deep breath and started over. "I wanted to tell you I'm sorry."

His heart pounded against his chest. "You did?"

Lucas would've been fine with simply agreeing to forget the past two days and start over. After all, there was a lot he was sorry about, too. But now that she'd said the words, they were like a balm, healing him bone-deep.

"For lashing out." She nodded and started walking slowly toward the stairs while she kept talking. "You've been amazing with my kids all summer."

Her eyes danced as she set her foot on the first step. "Okay, maybe not when we first got here—but mostly amazing."

"Thank you." He laughed. "I think?"

"I was wrong about you," she said, slowly climbing up the stairs while he moved down them, toward the landing.

Once there, he paused and waited for her to meet him in the middle. After all, wasn't that their thing? "You were?"

"Maybe I wanted to be right, but you were just kind of…"

"Great?" he said.

She stepped onto the landing and closed the remaining the distance between them. Then she was suddenly right there, close enough for Lucas to catch the scent of her wind-tossed hair. It smelled like orange blossoms and sugared coconut, and it made him want to kiss her until summer turned to fall.

"Kinda." Her smile radiated joy.

There was only one thing left to tell her, and he needed to do it now. They'd come too far to leave anything else left unsaid.

"So you don't think that I'm a stubborn, messy surfer who's totally distracted?" He arched a brow.

Jenna rolled her beautiful eyes. "Oh, you're absolutely stubborn and..."

And?

She stared at him. "Wait. How are you quoting...?"

"The message you left for the rental agency?"

She blew out a breath as realization dawned. "You're LM Management?" Then she swallowed, and Lucas traced the motion up and down the graceful column of her throat. "And you own the duplex."

"Hey, summer camp isn't a year-round gig. I had to diversify," he teased.

But she still looked embarrassed, and Lucas didn't want that. He didn't want her to wish he hadn't overheard the things she'd said. He just wanted her not to believe them anymore.

So he fixed his gaze with hers and told her the one thought he'd kept coming back to over and over, even when he'd worried he might never see her again. "I'm really glad that you stayed."

She brightened. "I didn't mean all those things I said."

That wasn't the whole truth, and they both knew it. She'd made her disdain for his freewheeling, houseplant-free lifestyle more than clear in the beginning. They'd both been wrong about a lot of things back then.

She shrugged. "Okay, maybe I did when I first said it, but I was wrong."

He nodded. "I was, too."

"You were?" she breathed.

Without a doubt. He'd been so terribly misguided, so thoroughly foolish about the most important thing of all. "I was wrong to think I could stay unattached to the three of you."

It was important for him to make that clear. He didn't just have feelings for Jenna— he loved Ally and Nick too. Although he suspected that Jenna had recognized how thoroughly he'd fallen for them even before he'd even been aware of it himself.

"Why do think I'm still hanging around here?" Had she actually believed he'd go anywhere without telling them goodbye? "You got me."

She blinked furiously, but it didn't stop her eyes from welling up. "What about your trip?"

"Don't worry about that. I'll catch up. I just couldn't miss you." He drew in a long breath, and he thought about the tie Jenna had given him after dinner a few nights ago and the look of pride on Ally and Nick's faces when he'd opened it. That was the moment when Lucas had known they'd stolen his heart, the moment when everything changed.

No matter how hard he'd tried not to believe it. "*All* of you."

She smiled through a thick veil of tears.

"Are you crying?"

"*No,*" she said as more tears streamed down her face. "Why does everyone keep saying that?"

"Come here." He reached for her, pulling her close, and just like that, it felt like every part of Lucas's life clicked into place.

"What? I'm not crying," she murmured into his shoulder.

"I know," he whispered. If she wanted to pretend she was in control, he'd let her...

So long as she was his.

"What are we going to do?" she said, her voice equal parts wonder and worry.

He ran a soothing hand up and down her back. "About all of this?"

"About *us*?"

He pulled back just far enough to meet her gaze. Then he tucked her hair behind her ear and mustered as much solemnity as he possibly could. "First, I think we need to set some new rules. You know, guidelines."

"Oh." A smile tugged at her lips before she nodded in mock seriousness. "And what would those guidelines look like, exactly?"

"Rule number one, I definitely get to kiss you." That was a biggie, far more important than no music after 9 p.m. or making sure

Tank kept all four of his paws on Lucas's side of the patio.

"Like right now?" A slow smile crept to her lips.

Like yesterday. Lucas nodded. "Preferably."

"I'm willing to agree to that," she said, all-business.

But when he cupped her face in his hands, the pretense fell away, leaving nothing but love behind. Love...

And the most perfect kiss Lucas could ever want—sweet like honey from the moment his lips touched hers. Alive and wistful, all at the same time. It had taken them a long, long time to get to this place, and now that they'd found their way, he never wanted to leave. Jenna and her kids were his heart.

His *home.*

And he no longer wanted that home split down the middle.

He rested his forehead against Jenna's as her heartbeat crashed into his. "Now I've got one more rule that needs to be addressed."

The sun dipped beneath the horizon, spilling rose-gold light over the sea as Jenna made her way over the dune with a few planks from the recently disassembled fence balanced in her hands.

Ally, Nick and Lucas walked along the

sand beside her with the remaining boards split between them. Tearing down the dividing line that had separated the two halves of the beach house for five weeks straight had been a group effort. And now watching the last remaining bits of the fence burn into ash would be one too.

"So there are no sides anymore?" Nick asked as they cleared the sea oats and carried the wood toward the bonfire pit.

"You are free to roam," Lucas said.

Ally glanced at him over her shoulder. "Does that mean Tank can come over whenever he wants?"

He answered her with a smile. "Only if I can come over with him."

Good answer, Jenna thought. Perfect answer, actually. She just wished she would've had the courage to tear down the fence weeks ago, when they'd only been halfway through their chocolate supply and the summer wasn't nearly over.

Better late than never and all that, but she wasn't ready to go. Not even close.

She glanced to her left—toward the place where Lucas had just been walking alongside her—but his steps had slowed so that he was now walking in step with Nick. Their conversation instantly made her throat thick with emotion.

"Hey, I'm sorry I let you down, bud. It was my bad," Lucas said.

"That's okay." Nick's voice was upbeat.

In light of his tone, Jenna expected Lucas to drop the subject.

He didn't. "No, it isn't. But I promise to make it up to you."

Jenna snuck a glance at them just as Nick stopped walking to grin up at Lucas. "I'd like that."

Lucas's brows rose "Yeah?"

"Yeah."

Then for what felt like the millionth time, Jenna's eyes stung with tears as Lucas shifted the wood he was carrying to one arm so he could wrap the other around Nick's shoulders. She really needed to get a grip on the crying situation, but maybe she'd let it go just this once.

She was finally allowing herself to feel again. To *be*. She just hadn't realized it would be such a weepy process.

"You realize we're hugging, right?" Nick said.

"Yup. And we're good." Lucas gave him one last squeeze before releasing his hold on Nick's shoulders.

Jenna waited for them to catch up, pausing at the edge of the fire pit to admire the waves, tipped pink by the blazing sunset.

She'd miss this place.

She'd miss feeling the sand between her toes and the salty taste of the ocean on her lips. She'd miss the sound of gulls crying overhead and moonlit waves as the background music to her late-night writing sessions. She'd miss Tank's scruffy face and his jaunty little trot.

But she'd miss her neighbor most of all.

"All right, throw it in," she said.

In unison, they tossed the wood into the fire and stepped back to watch the flames lick higher.

Good riddance.

Ally challenged Nick to a race back to the house, and in a flash they were gone, leaving Jenna and Lucas alone with everything that had once stood between them now lying in a pile at their feet. In the distance, she could hear the laughter of her children and Tank's happy yips, and joy blossomed inside her.

Lucas slipped his arm around her waist. She leaned into him, resting her head against his shoulder.

"I don't want this summer to end." She whispered so quietly that the ocean should have swallowed her words, but Lucas still heard them.

"It doesn't have to."

Jenna sighed. "Yeah, it kind of does. We have to head back tomorrow."

"What if your rental agent said you could stay longer?" There was a smile in his voice, and it made her laugh.

"That's sweet, but logistically..." She started to rattle off a list of reasons why their relationship was doomed to fail, but then she stopped herself.

Because what if it wasn't? What if the fence was truly gone for good?

"We'll make a plan," he said with a nod.

She *did* have a certain fondness for plans. She liked them almost as much as she liked neatly organized bins, cozy cardigans, and beating Lucas at beach volleyball.

She peered up at him. "You think we can make this work?"

"We made the last five weeks work. We can make *this* work." He spun her around to face him and brushed her hair from her eyes with gentle fingers. "Now, I have one more question for you."

"Okay." She searched his gaze, looking for a hint of what was to come.

"Can we go back to rule number one?"

The kissing rule.

Her knees turned to water, and she smiled wide. "Yes, please."

And as the surfer-next-door kissed Jenna Turner again, with her feet in the sand and her heart on her sleeve, she thought about new beginnings instead of endings and how sometimes a story's sequel could be even better than its opening act. Most of all, she thought about the dog days of summer and these past few cherished weeks on the island, her favorite summer at the shore.

Epilogue

*L*UCAS MARRIED JENNA ON A crisp autumn day—the time of year when the sea turtle nests on Tybee Island hatch, spilling tiny baby turtles onto the shore to make their way home.

The wedding took place exactly a year and one month from the date they'd torn down the fence, in a modest church overlooking the sea. Ally made the groom's cake— triple chocolate, of course—and Nick walked his mother down the aisle. There wasn't a dry eye in the house, except maybe Tank's. His tail wagged throughout the entire ceremony, leaving him so exhausted that he napped his way through the reception. Which was really a shame, because Ally had been training him for weeks to catch the bouquet.

Maureen and Ian offered to keep the kids so Lucas could whisk Jenna away on a private honeymoon, but it didn't feel right. There would be time for that later when Nick and Ally went to visit their dad. Lucas hadn't only married Jenna—he'd chosen them all, and starting a new life *together* seemed important.

So the night after he said "I do," Lucas stood alongside his three favorite people, licking ice cream cones while they waited for a fireworks show to start.

"Are you cold?" he asked when he spied Jenna performing a one-handed buttoning maneuver on her cardigan. The woman had some serious mom skills, but he'd known that since day one.

"I'm perfect." She grinned at him, then frowned down at her cherry vanilla. "But remind me whose idea it was to get ice cream on a cool night like this."

"Ally's," Lucas said in unison with Nick.

She really needed to ask?

"Ice cream is a year-round treat." Ally bounced on her toes.

"If you say so," Nick countered. Lucas couldn't help but notice he'd ordered a double-scoop though, so it wasn't as if he objected.

"It's really good ice cream, I have to admit." Jenna took a bite and came away with a dollop of pink cream on the tip of her nose.

Lucas laughed and motioned toward her face with his cone. "You've got a little something there."

"Oh yeah?" Her brows lifted, and he had a feeling he knew what was coming.

He was right, because before he could

find an escape route in the crowded park, she reached over and dabbed his nose with her ice cream.

Ally and Nick collapsed into giggles. There was only one way to win a battle like this one, so Lucas pulled his wife close and gave her a big, smacking kiss. Both of them were sticky messes now, but neither cared.

Ally said, "Only one thing could make this night better."

Jenna and Lucas exchanged a glance.

"What's that?" Lucas asked. He genuinely wanted to know because, as moments went, this one was pretty perfect.

"If Tank was here." Ally straightened the mouse ears on her head and took a generous lick of her ice cream cone. "Obviously."

Lucas laughed.

Obviously!

The kid had a point. It wasn't truly a vacation without his dog, which was precisely why Tank was cozied up at their Florida beach condo rental just a short tram ride away from Cinderella's castle.

"Ally, honey. I don't think they allow dogs at Disney World," Jenna said as she slipped her hand into Lucas's.

Behind her, Lucas could see flying elephants and a haunted castle high up on a hill. Somewhere nearby, a roller coaster whirled past and Nick's eyes lit up. Lucas was Nick's ride-buddy. If it rocked, rolled, dropped you from an immense height, spun you around or spit you back out, they'd been on it. In most instances, twice. Lucas thanked his lucky stars that a lifetime of being on the water had prepared him for the motion-sickness challenge that came with being a dad.

Meanwhile, he wouldn't be surprised if Ally was silently planning a petition to allow dogs into the park. He wouldn't be surprised if she succeeded.

He shot her a smile. "It's okay because Tank isn't really a theme park dog."

Jenna's gaze met his, then she glanced at his head and her lips twitched into a smile. Yes, much to everyone's amusement, Lucas was wearing mouse ears. If he was going to Disney World on his honeymoon, he was go-ing *all in*. Kayla had demanded a selfie, and Lucas playfully refused. But he was pretty sure Jenna had already snuck a photo be-hind his back and sent it along. Lucas fully expected it to be blown up and hanging in a frame at the summer camp next season.

The camp on Tybee Island was now known as the flagship summer camp. Three others had been opened along the Georgia coast, and Lucas and his partners were thinking about expanding into the Outer Banks area of the Carolinas next.

"I know Tank isn't a theme park dog," Ally said as if it were a well-documented fact.

Nick looked down at his sister. He'd grown like a weed over the past year and spent most of his time at the pool with Grayson, where Nick had successfully made the school swim team. This year, he'd be swimming for the junior high on Tybee Island, where Lucas was converting the duplex into one large beach house with room for the whole family. "What kind of dog is he, then?"

Ally shrugged. "Tank is a *family* dog."

Jenna squeezed Lucas's hand tight and a feeling so good, so pure filled his chest that he imagined this is what it must feel like to catch the biggest monster wave the ocean had to offer.

A family dog.

He smiled to himself in the cool moonlight.

Then the first firework of the night boomed overhead, illuminating the sky in glittering violets, aquas and blues—dazzling beach colors that reminded Lucas of the sea and the shore, and of the summer he lost his heart to the beautiful woman standing beside him and the two best kids in the entire world.

But he really hadn't lost his heart, had he? He'd found it, and then just like Tank, everything about his life had changed.

If Tank was a family dog, then that made Lucas a family man. And he was perfectly fine with that.

Shrimp Scampi

A Hallmark Original Recipe

"We'll take a whole crab, some of your garlic shrimp, two rolls and a whole stack of napkins!" That's how Lucas places the order at the little beachside shrimp shack when he takes Jenna out for the first time. You can create that same vacation atmosphere at home with our Shrimp Scampi recipe. Dress it up with a little thin spaghetti, as we did, or dress it down with a red checkered tablecloth and a bottle of wine on your back porch. Either way, plan your own romantic escape with this easy one-pan recipe.

Yield: 4 servings
Prep Time: 40 minutes
Cook Time: 20 minutes
Total Time: 60 minutes

INGREDIENTS

- 1-pound large shrimp, peeled and deveined, (21-25 pieces per pound), thawed if frozen
- 1 tablespoon extra-virgin olive oil
- 2 garlic cloves, minced
- 1 teaspoon kosher salt
- ½ pound thin spaghetti, uncooked
- 2 tablespoons extra-virgin olive oil
- 3 garlic cloves, thin-sliced
- ¼ teaspoon crushed red pepper flakes
- ½ cup dry white wine
- 2 tablespoons fresh squeezed lemon juice
- 4 tablespoons unsalted butter
- 2 cups fresh spinach leaves, trimmed, lightly packed
- ½ teaspoon coarse-ground black pepper
- As needed, fresh lemon wedges
- 2 tablespoons shaved Parmesan

DIRECTIONS

1. Drain shrimp, pat dry and remove tails, if desired.

2. Combine shrimp, 1 tablespoon olive oil, minced garlic and salt in a bowl and toss to evenly coat. Refrigerate for 20 to 30 minutes.

3. While shrimp is marinating, bring a large pot of salted water to a boil. Add

spaghetti and cook for 6 to 7 minutes or until cooked al dente. Drain; keep warm.

4. Heat 2 tablespoons olive oil in a large skillet over medium heat; add marinated shrimp and cook just until shrimp turn pink (about 2 minutes), stirring frequently. Using a slotted spoon, transfer shrimp to a bowl and reserve.

5. Add sliced garlic and crushed red pepper flakes to skillet and sauté over medium-low heat for 1 minute, stirring frequently. Add white wine and lemon juice; simmer until liquid is reduced by half. Add butter and whisk over medium-low heat until butter is melted and sauce is fully blended.

6. Add spinach, black pepper and reserved shrimp to skillet; sauté briefly to fully cook shrimp and wilt spinach, stirring frequently.

7. Add spaghetti to skillet and lightly toss to blend. Divide shrimp scampi evenly between 4 bowls. Garnish with fresh lemon slices and shaved Parmesan.

Thanks so much for reading *Love at the Shore*!

You might also enjoy these other books from Hallmark Publishing:

The Story of Us
Beach Wedding Weekend
A Simple Wedding
Country Hearts
Love on Location
Sunrise Cabin

For information about our new releases and exclusive offers, sign up for our free newsletter!

You can also connect with us here:

Facebook.com/HallmarkPublishing

Twitter.com/HallmarkPublish

About the Author

Teri Wilson is the *Publishers Weekly* bestselling author/creator of the Hallmark Channel
Original Movies *Unleashing Mr. Darcy*, *Mar-
rying Mr. Darcy*, *The Art of Us*, and *Northern
Lights of Christmas*, based on her book *Sleigh
Bell Sweethearts*. She is also a recipient of
the prestigious RITA Award for excellence in
romantic fiction. Teri has a major weakness
for cute animals, pretty dresses and Audrey
Hepburn films, and she loves following the
British royal family.

Visit her at www.teriwilson.net or on Twitter
@TeriWilsonauthr.